Trap Gyrl 2

By Barbie Scott

D1711270

Chapter 1

Cash & Carter

"Where am I?" I asked myself while looking around the unfamiliar room I was in.

I then looked down at my shoulder that was draped in bandages and wondered why was my head pounding.

"What the fuck happened? Where am I?"

I tried to lift up off the small twin sized bed but failed because of the pain. I tried to scream but my throat was sore so my screams were distinctive.

Boom! all of a sudden, the door flung open.

I stared at the man that I never thought I'd see again, Carter. My mind was racing, my heart was pounding, and at any moment, I thought I'd wake up from the dream I was having.

Me and Carter stared at each other for what seemed like an eternity. His oval shaped hazel eyes told an entire story. He appeared to be in some sort of trance and didn't utter one word. I tried to lift up again, breaking him from his train of thoughts. He ran over to my bedside and again, I was stuck in a zone, gazing into his eyes.

"Where's Brooklyn? Oh my God, Carter, what's going on? How long have I been here?" I asked the moment I regain my composure to speak. The tears began to fall from my eyes but not because I was in pain but because I didn't understand what the fuck was going on.

It all began to come back to me. I remembered being held captive by Ricky, then next thing I knew, he was laying in a pool of blood. I remembered I was shot, then I passed out but before I drifted off, I came face to face with Carter. I remember talking to Brooklyn and hearing Pedro screaming in the background. Oh my God, Pedro. I thought to myself and began to cry harder.

"Cash, please stop crying, ma," Carter said, sitting down on the bed beside me.

"Carter, what's going on? I mean, you're supposed to be dead. It's been years and you're standing in front of me talking bout don't cry. I don't know if this a dream or reality. Are you a ghost?" I began to cry harder.

Carter looked at me with pitiful eyes but remained quiet. This shit was starting to piss me off. I had so many questions, I needed answers and this nigga was mute.

"I'm sorry, Cash. But I have my reasons," he turned away then dropped his head. "You got shot and you were in a coma for almost three weeks," he said. He lifted me off the bed and began pacing the room.

I looked at him and he looked so much like Brooklyn, all I could do was shake my head and cry.

"Three weeks?" I mumbled under my breath. "Do you know I'm with Brooklyn now?" I looked at him with the most pleading eyes. "But I didn't know he was your…"

Before I could finish he cut me off. "Yes, I know you are with my brother," he said with his face frowned up. "But did you really know he was my brother, though, Cash? And don't lie, ma!"

"No, I swear I didn't know. If I had known, I wouldn't have fucked with him, Carter," I sighed heavily and put my head down.

"Do you love him?" he asked like he desperately wanted to know the answer. But I couldn't lie, I had to tell him. I loved Brook to death and we had built something indescribable, therefore, sooner or later, he would know the truth.

"Yes! Yes, I love him," again, I put my head down.

He lifted my chin to force me to look at him but when I dropped my head again, he just watched me with ease. He began rubbing his hands through his long dreads and shook his head, repeatedly.

"I've been following you, ma. When I surfaced for the first time, I pulled up to your house and saw you and Brooklyn getting in your car," as he spoke, it all started to make sense. "I had noticed someone following me numerous of times but I brushed it off.

"That's how I knew you were at the warehouse. I saw you being led to a van with a blindfold on, coming out your crib so I followed to the location."

"But why, Carter? Why all this time?" I asked. This nigga had some explaining to do so I shot him a look that said get to talking.

6

"Man, what's up with that nigga Que?" he asked, avoiding my question. Fuck that, why was Que even a factor in what I had asked?

"Que is now in jail, but I'm asking you a question, so what the fuck does Que have to do with anything?"

Carter stared at me again with tranquilizing eyes and boy was this man still sexy. He had gotten thicker like he'd spent his entire time away doing pushups. His dreads had grown much longer and the once thin gold tee was now full.

I shook off any thoughts of him and focused on my question at hand. I was now in love with Brooklyn and he was just as fine, which reminded me I needed to use the phone.

"Can I use the phone, please? I know people think I'm dead and I'm sure Brook is worried sick about me," I asked, shamefully.

He looked at me with an uneasy look before he spoke.

"I'ma take you to him," he said right before storming out of the room.

Brooklyn Nino

I stood at the door, shocked as hell. How the fuck am I about to tell this lady her that her only daughter is dead.

My heart hurt to the core because the love of my life was gone, and I felt like I failed her mother. I promised Ms. Lopez that I'd keep Cash safe, now, here her mother stood before me, fresh out of Federal penitentiary, and I had to be the bad new barrier.

"Yes, Ms. Lopez, it's me Brooklyn," I said, and she smiled lovingly. I opened the door further to let her in.

"My, you are fine," she reached out for a hug.

"Ms. Lopez, I have some bad news," I jumped straight to it. There was no need to hold the information from her because Cash was the reason she was here.

She gave me an uneasy look and all I could do was drop my head.

"Brooklyn, what's wrong? Is my baby ok? Where is she?" she asked, looking around as if any moment Cash would appear.

"She's dead, Ms. Lopez," I said just above a whisper.

She looked at me to see my reaction and when she saw I wasn't bullshitting, she dropped to her knees and began screaming. A single tear slid down my face, I was beyond hurt. Ms. Lopez was a powerful woman that ran the biggest drug empire in Miami. She bodied niggas in a heartbeat and here she stood before me with a million tears running down her face.

"What happened, Brook? Oh my God, what happened to my child?" she cried, hysterically.

"I'm so sorry, Ms. Lopez," was all I could say.

I helped her off the floor and led her to the couch. I sat beside her to console her and to my surprise, she put her head on my shoulder.

After giving Ms. Lopez some time to regain herself, I began telling her who was behind this madness that ruined both our lives.

9

"It was Al Jr."

"Al?"

"Yes, Big Al's son."

She looked at me with wide eyes and then shook her head.

"I still don't really know what happened. We had got into a fight so she stormed out and turned her phone off. A few hours later, one of my workers hit me to tell me Que had gotten knocked by twelve, so I immediately called Cash and her phone kept going straight to voicemail. I went to her house and shit was crazy because it was pitch black like the electricity was off, right then, I knew something was wrong. When I got inside the house, she was nowhere to be found but I found Pedro laying in a pool of blood out back."

"Oh my God, Pedro. Please tell me he's ok?" she asked and began to cry again.

"Yes, Pedro is fine, he's actually out back. I had him come stay with me for a while until he got better."

"Oh, thank God."

"So, while I was with my private doctor helping him with Pedro, I received a call from an unknown number. It was Lil Al's bitch ass requesting money. Before I could agree to a location, I heard a single shot then Cash began screaming. After that, I heard several more shots and then, silence."

"Ohh, my God, oh, my God, my poor daughter. This is all my fault. I shouldn't have put her into this line of work. This is all my fault, Brooklyn," Ms. Lopez cried on my shoulder.

"I'm sorry too, Ms. Lopez. I feel like I failed you."

"No, no, it's not your fault, Brook. Please, don't beat yourself up, it's not your fault." She stood to her feet.

When I looked into her eyes, it was like I'd seen the devil himself. Ms. Lopez went from crying to straight gangsta mode so I knew shit was about to get ugly. She walked out the house and I was sure she was going to find Pedro.

Defeated I sat down on the couch and shook my head until it seemed as if any minute it would fall off. Shit was about to get ugly in these streets for Cash and I was ready.

11

Que

I've been sitting in this hell hole three weeks. I've contemplated suicide plenty times, but I knew   I had to be here for my daughter. I felt like I didn't want to live anymore since the news I got from Nino about Cash being dead. Cash was my world and without her, it was like what the fuck did I have left to live for? I regretted all the drama I put her through with Nino and Keisha, shit I regretted all the bitches I slept with because if only I had gotten my act together, Cash would have been wifey, for real. Now all I had was memories and punk as pictures that were taped on my wall beside my bunk.

As far as my case, shit was looking pretty good for me because the only evidence they had was the statement from Mike's bitch ass. Somehow, the work they copped from me using Mike as an informant had vanished from the evidence room right along with the fucking bug he was wearing. I knew it could have only been one person that could make that kind of call… Ms. Lopez. It was a trip how powerful that lady was, even behind the walls.

Diane had played a big part in it as well. The judge was her good friend from college so all we had to do was slide him a mill ticket, which wasn't shit. Next, we had to get a hold of Mike's bitch ass, and Blaze assured me that he would find him. The pigs had Mike stashed away in Protective Custody but with Marcus and Diane having inside connects, I knew it would be easy getting to his bitch ass. My first time appearing in court, the judge revoked my bail. I had another court date in three months, I just prayed Diane would get me a bond. Because this was federal court, they only gave you court dates every three months so I didn't have a choice but to sit in this bitch and wait.

I used the phone to call Nina and check up on her but all she did was cry, so I quickly hung up the phone with her. I was already stressed enough because I was in this bitch, and Nina wasn't making my situation any better. I had about another fifteen minutes left to use the phone so I called Nino to check up on him. After all the bullshit that's been going on, Nino and I became pretty close. I hated the drama I put him and Cash through because he was actually a cool nigga.

"Hello," Nino answered and immediately pushed five to connect the call.

13

"What's the word, nigga?"

"Man, you ain't gonna believe this shit…"

"What happened now, man?" I asked, praying it wasn't any more bad news.

"Nigga, Ms. Lopez is out!"

"What!" I shouted through the phone. I couldn't believe what Nino was saying.

"Hell yeah, man. She popped up at my door this morning."

"Damn! Did you tell her?"

"Yeah, shit, I had to…"

"So, how is she taking it?"

"She broke down at first, then switched up on me with eyes of a straight killa," he boasted and we both laughed.

"Damn. So where she at now?"

"She out back with Pedro right now, you wanna holler at her?"

14

"Honestly, nah. I'm not ready yet," I said, shaking my head. As bad as I needed to holla at Ms. Lopez, I just couldn't bring myself to do it.

"I feel you, shit. So, how you holding up?"

"I'm doing a lot better. Aye, I need you to take Keisha some dough for me, man. Blaze crazy ass ain't answer his phone."

"Aight, fasho, I got you."

"Good looking, man. Just call my phone when you on your way, she got it."

"Haha. What, nigga? Ah, I know she then called every last bitch in that muthafucka," Nino said, causing us to both laughed again.

"Man, every time I call that bitch, she tripping about a different bitch. Aye, the phone bout to hang up, tho', so handle that for me, Nino, I appreciate it. I'll call and talk to Ms. Lopez in a couple days, alright?"

"Alright, my nigga, stay up."

"One…"

"One…" I hung up and went back to my cell.

I laid on my bunk and began reading. It seemed like this was the only time a nigga read, but shit, it made time fly.

Chapter 2

Cash

I got up out the bed and headed into the foyer to find Carter. He was sitting on the couch, smoking a blunt. I wasn't a smoker but the way I was feeling, some good ganja was needed. Carter was so wrapped up in his thoughts, he didn't even see me standing there. I watched him as he puffed on the rolled blunt and admired how fine he looked in a simple white t-shirt and some gray KMK sweats. The more I watched him, the more I missed Brook. The last conversation we had was heated because I had just found out that they were brothers, but I knew at this point, he wasn't even stressing it.

I walked over to the couch and took a seat beside him but moving slowly because of my wombs. He passed me the blunt, I took two hits and instantly began coughing.

"You still an amateur?" he said, causing me to laugh a little.

I didn't even reply, I just took another hit and passed it back to him.

"So, why didn't you tell me you were married, Carter?" I asked as if I didn't care, but deep down inside, it bothered me.

He looked at me and shook his head a few times before speaking.

"To be honest, ma, me and Lydia wasn't even together when I was fucking with you. After the night I saw you with ol boy at the restaurant, I had finally gone back home. I hadn't been to see my kids in days so I said fuck it. You know, you fucked a nigga up with that move you pulled."

"I'ma be honest too. I didn't think you were into me like that, Carter."

"Cash, you were my Gutta Baby. I was ready to wife yo ass," he said and his words made me feel worse than before.

"I'm sorry, Carter."

18

"It's alright, ma," he smiled.

Carter looked at me with the most lustful eyes and it was like Deja Vu. He then leaned over and kissed me. I parted my lips to let his tongue explore mine and right at that moment, all the feelings I had for him came rushing back through my body.

Brooklyn, I thought to myself and pulled back.

"I'm sorry, Carter, we can't do this."

He stood up and gazed at me, then walked out. He left me alone, drowning in my own thoughts. I sighed deeply and stood to my feet. He looked kind of upset but this nigga had so much explaining to do. Not only to me but to Brooklyn and his wife so I brushed his ass off.

Right now, I needed to see Brook because I was feeling guilty as hell. I needed to get out of this house as soon as possible. I had to make sure Pedro was ok and I needed to talk to my mother. I didn't know how Brook would react to me popping up to his door with Carter, but I had to get back to the real world. Not to mention, I needed to check on Que and get a hold of this nigga Mike so I could send him home to his maker. I had a drug empire to run and I was more than sure my girls were dying inside without me.

After about an hour, Carter came back into the living room with a pair of crutches and Nike flip flops. He slid the shoes onto my feet then helped me lift up, handing me one crutch at a time. After getting myself together, I walked slowly through the giant house. When we made it to the front door, I could tell we were nowhere near home so I stopped in my tracks to look at Carter.

"Where are we?"

"Brazil," Carter responded but kept straight.

Brazil? I thought to myself and giggled because this nigga was on some real Macavelli type shit.

When we made it outside, I had to cover my eyes from the ray of the sun that nearly blinded me. A car pulled up, which I assumed was the car that would be driving us to the airport.

When Carter opened the back door for me, a really beautiful woman sat pretty in the back. I was more than sure it was one of Carter's Brazilian bimbos. A sense of jealousy crept upon me and now I was really ready to get back to my man. No lie, she was breathtaking. She had a really pretty face and her body was to die for.

This scanless muthafucka, I thought to myself shaking my head.

Carter must have sensed my attitude because he had an uneasy look on his face. The bitch spoke to me and I simply waved her off and through her a head nod. I climbed into the back seat and I didn't have shit else to say for the remainder of the ride. I knew I was being childish but this nigga was just trying to make out with me, he had a wife at home, and here he was with his Brazilian bitch.

Niggas!

Looking at Carter, I could tell he was still somehow getting money. The home we were in was huge and I was now sitting in the backseat of a Fathom. I gazed out the window in deep thought. I had so many different emotions running through my body. I didn't know if I should cry, scream or laugh. Just thinking about my life in just these last six months was enough to write a book. I had been shot twice, lost a baby, one of my top Lieutenants was snitching, and I was sitting in the backseat with my once lover, who I thought was dead, and his mistress. Shit couldn't get any crazier.

After the long nine-hour flight on Carter's private jet, I was beyond tired and ready to get away from him and this bitch, with her irritating accent.

I was nervous as hell on the drive to Brook's house but I had to suck it up. We pulled up to a hotel and I was puzzled to find out why were we here. Carter hopped out, followed by his bimbo. He gave her a peck on the lips, then she sashayed into the hotel without a care in the world.

He had to stash his little bitch, I thought to myself, laughing. Niggas ain't shit and Carter was in that same boat.

When we pulled up to Brooklyn's home, I noticed a limo out front. I was sure it wasn't Brook's because he had a Maybach with a driver and he never rode in limos. I jumped out the car so fast that you wouldn't have even thought I was shot. I took a deep breath and slowly walked up to the front door.

Through the tiny glass windows, I could see a female figure lying on the sofa. I instantly got heated. It had only been a little over three weeks and this nigga had already moved on. As bad as I wanted to leave, I had to make my presence known.

I politely let myself into the home and the chick looked up at me in shock.

"Who are you and why the fuck you in my house?"

"Your house?"

"Yes, bitch, my house."

We began shouting at the top of our lungs. Bullet wombs or not, I was ready to whoop some ass. I got in the chick's face right when Carter came barging through the door.

"Breela?" Carter said like he knew her. Now I was puzzled.

"Bronx! Oh my gosh!" the chick shouted and began crying instantly.

Carter pulled her in for a hug right when I turned to him puzzled. I looked towards the kitchen area and I was beyond ecstatic.

"Mommy!" I yelled.

My mother stood there with Pedro by her side and wearing the biggest smile that would literally light the horizon. The tears began to fall like Niagara Falls, I was beyond speechless.

Brooklyn Nino

I pulled into Que's driveway and hopped out my whip. I headed to the door and knocked twice, waiting for Keisha to let me in. After a few more knocks, she finally made her way to the door. She had an awkward smile on her face but stood to the side so I could walk into her and Que's home. I went into my pocket and peeled off two stacks, handing them to her. She was smiling from ear to ear through glassy eyes like she had been drinking a little too much. I looked around the living room, trying to see where the fuck was the baby because she looked a little too saucy for me.

"Where's the baby, Keisha?"

"She's with my mom."

"Oh, ok. Well, if you need some more money, hit me up," I said, handing her the stacks.

As I proceeded to walk out, she grabbed my arm. "Why you leaving so soon?" she asked, tugging at my belt buckle.

I quickly backed up and she wasn't giving up. This bitch buggin, yo.

"What's good with you, ma? You straight?"

"I want you, Brooklyn," she said and dropped to her knees, trying to unfasten my belt right when my phone rang.

"Hello?"

"Brooklyn, get home now!" Ms. Lopez said through the phone.

"Is everything ok, Ms. Lopez?"

"Yes, I just need you here, ASAP."

"I'm on my way," I hung up.

I was so caught into my phone conversation, I didn't even realize this bitch had my dick out and was about to stick it in her mouth.

I pushed her back and then fixed my clothing. "Bitch, you foul," I shook my head.

"I want you, Brooklyn. Why are you tripping? Cash is dead and Que in jail, I won't tell nobody," she spat.

26

I just shook my head for the tenth time. Once a thot, always a thot, I thought to myself.

This wasn't my get down. I would never disrespect Cash, dead or alive and for sure, I wasn't going to disrespect Que.

I jumped in my whip and turned on my Killa F from the Finatticz CD and jumped straight on the freeway. I couldn't get the thoughts of Keisha out my head. No matter how much me and Que beefed or the situation with Cash being pregnant by Que, I still wasn't that type of nigga. If it was one thing I believed in, that was Loyalty. Me and Que were now cool and the love of my life had been gone not even a full month.

When I finally made it home, I parked my ride and headed up the driveway. I was so puzzled to why Ms. Lopez had called me in such a frantic. I reached my front door and I could see a few people standing in my living room. I opened the door and was caught dead in my tracks. What the fuck! I was ready to pass out. This couldn't be real.

Cash stood off to the side with a look that I couldn't read. I looked from Cash to my fucking brother. All I know

27

is these muthafuckas had some explaining to do. I tilted my head to the side and crossed my arms over my chest. I didn't utter one word. I waited for one of the two to speak; straight up!

Blaze

"Ohhh shit, Blaze!"

"Yeah, ma, make that pussy talk to me."

"I'm bout to cum, oh my God. I'm about to cum, bae!"

"Cum for daddy, ma. Cum for daddy, then," I told Tiny as she came all over my dick. I wasn't even done but I didn't bug her because she looked worn out.

I rolled off her, then she laid her head on my chest, breathing hard. I rubbed my hands through her long hair and kissed her on the forehead. Tiny and I had been fucking three straight hours. No lie, for as many kids she had, she had some good as pussy.

Ever since Cash had died, Tiny and I became closer than before. Since her bitch ass husband was a snitch and we already crept before, we rekindled our affair after shit got rough in these streets. At first, I didn't trust her, but she blew my phone up for the hundredth time, I had finally answered. She cried to me about how Mike hadn't been home and she thought something was up with him because the few times she had seen him, he was acting paranoid. Little did she know, there was a lot up with that nigga.

I invited her to my crib and when she showed up on my doorstep, I caved in. We both were going through it over Cash's death so we consoled each other, then one thing led to the next. I've been sick without Cash to the point I wanted to get out the game but Que needed me, and not only him, Ms. Lopez needed us the most.

I rolled over and checked my phone that had rung at least ten times, back to back. It was Nino, so I quickly dialed his number, knowing something wasn't right. After four rings, he finally answered.

"Nino, what's the deal, my nigga?"

"Man, come to my crib now, you ain't gonna believe this shit."

"You straight, man?" I asked. His background was loud as hell and I could've sworn I heard Cash's voice. I quickly shook it off, knowing Cash was resting with her angles. "I'm on my way, Nino," I said, lifting up to put my clothes on.

30

"Aight, man," Nino responded, sounding like he was stressed the fuck out.

"Where are you going?" Tiny asked, upset because her quality time was coming to an end.

"Something came up at Nino's."

"I'm going too, you not leaving me," she shot me.

I huffed a little, but I kind of got aroused at how Tiny was becoming my ride or die.

"Come on, ma. Hurry up, though, because it sounded important."

She ran into the restroom, I assumed she was going to wipe up. She walked out with a wash cloth and began cleaning my dick. She then went back into the restroom, so I finished dressing and waited for her to finish.

We hopped in my ride and headed over to Nino's in full speed. I was feeling kind of weird because this would be me and Tiny's first appearance out in the streets together. Fuck it!

When we got out the car, I grabbed her hand because I could tell she was nervous. At this point, it was us against everybody. Tiny had been at my crib every day since she showed up at my doorstep. She made a nigga feel good like no woman has ever made me feel in a long time.

Anybody that knew me, knew I was the type of nigga that wouldn't let a bitch get close to me because of trust issues. Another nigga didn't have shit to do with it, it was more so I didn't trust bitches because they were setup artist. I was a real gunner when it came to bodying shit but I also saw a lot of niggas getting caught with their pants down. Ms. Lopez's empire was too much to play with so I got a little pussy here and there, but kept my feelings in my pockets.

Tiny and I walked to Brooklyn's door hand in hand and when I reached for the nob, I stopped in my tracks at what I saw before me. Cash? Ms. Lopez? What the fuck is going on? I thought as I made my way into the home. Carter? I blinked my eyes, knowing a nigga was having a bad dream, but nah, this shit was indeed reality.

Chapter 3

Cash

I ran into the arms of my mother. I was so ecstatic that I buried my head into her shoulder and cried my poor eyes out. I was caught between tears of joy and tears of being overwhelmed. It seemed like so much was going on. My mother began rubbing my back, and all she kept saying was, "Stop crying, Cash." It seemed like the more she said it, the harder I cried. When I felt the tears hit my shoulder, I looked up, my mother was crying too. She began examining my body like as if everything at this point wasn't real. When I smiled at her, she smiled back and we were now joyful.

Before I could speak, the door came flying open. The butterflies in my stomach seemed to worsen the moment Brooklyn walked in. I was so happy to see him but I knew I had some explaining to do. But first, these niggas had some explaining to do as to whom was this bitch

33

standing here. The look that Brooklyn wore let me know that he had a million and one questions. He crossed his arms over his chest and that was confirmation that someone needed to start talking.

I broke the stare down by running into Brook's arms and planting a kiss on his tender lips. I missed him so much. I kissed him over and over as he wrapped his arms around my waist. To my surprise, he didn't object, he simply kissed me back and then a smile crept across his face. Carter began to speak and the moment he opened his mouth, the smile Brook wore was wiped away. Brooklyn stared at his brother in shock. It looked as if so much was running through his mind, he didn't know what to ask first.

Brooklyn walked up to his brother and hugged him tightly, almost squeezing the life out of him. When I looked up, a suspicious grin crept across my face when Blaze and Tiny had walked into the home, hand in hand.

"Cash! Oh my God, Cash!" Tiny shouted and ran over to me. She as well began crying hysterically, causing me to cry again.

Blaze and I stared at each other for what seemed like a lifetime. He shook his head repeatedly, then pulled out his phone. I looked at him puzzled as he dialed a number, then my lips spread widely when I heard who he was talking to.

"Yo, Nina, get to Nino's house, ASAP, ma," Blaze said into the phone.

We couldn't hear what Nina was saying, so all we got was one end of the conversation.

"Naw, everything good, ma. Just get over here now. Yeah, ok. Well, tell her to hold off, trust me th e boutique could wait, ma," Blaze said, not taking his eyes off me.

When he hung up the phone, I put my hands on my hips and rolled my neck like a ghetto girl, waiting for him to bring his ass over to me. He then came over to me and hugged me, putting me in a headlock and playfully punched me on the top of my head. He then pulled me into his arms and for the first time in life, I saw Blaze cry. The single tear that slid down his face caused me to cry again and what shocked me most was Brooklyn had a tear in his eyes.

"Cash, you got niggas in here crying like little bitches and shit, ma," Blaze said, causing us all to laugh.

I looked over at Carter, he had the strange girl nestled in his arms. Brook must've sensed something because he looked at the two, then back at me.

"Cash, this is me and Bronx's little sister, Breela. Bree, this Cash, my lady," Brook said with a smile.

"I'm sorry," I said, running over to give her a hug and she hugged me back, smiling.

"It's ok…"

I walked over to take a seat because my arm was starting to bother me. Brooklyn and Carter both ran to my side and this shit was awkward as hell. Carter reached into his pocket and pulled out my pain medicine and when Brooklyn took notice, he ran to the kitchen and came back seconds later with a bottled water. He took a seat beside me, it was time for me and Carter to explain what had happened.

Carter spoke every detail about him following me and rescuing me from Ricky. He also explained why he'd been hiding out for so many years. I listened closely as he explained the situation with the Carlito Cartel that caused him to fake his death. After he was done, I understood why he'd did it because the Cartel wasn't one to fuck with. I

36

could tell there was a piece of the story missing but I left it alone because if he wanted us to know, he would have told it.

Carter and Brooklyn went outside to talk amongst each other. Blaze and Tiny were cuddled in the corner, indulged in their own conversation. They actually looked cute together. Tiny little self barely came to Blaze's shoulder as his six foot, seven inch frame towered her. My mother, Pedro, and I sat on the sofa and caught up on everything that had been going on and she explained to us how she had gotten out sooner than her release date. From the look Pedro wore, I could tell all along he knew she was coming home.

Nina

I drove as fast as I could to Nino's crib. Whatever Blaze had wanted, it sounded very important. I was in the middle of deciding on patterns for my boutique's grand opening but I was sure this was more important.

I named the boutique "Nina Cash" after my now deceased best friend. Ever since the passing of Cash, I was so distraught that I almost gave up on life. Nino encouraged me to keep going with the boutique because Cash would have been so proud of me. He also gave me the keys to her all-female barbershop "Trap Gyrl" and told me to open it up when I was ready. We were more than sure Que would walk away Scott-free from his drug case so we were gonna let him run her night club called "Juice."

My stomach began to do somersaults. I didn't know if it was because of the way Blaze had called me or was it because of my baby. Yes, you heard right. I was pregnant as hell and already miserable. I was only three months but I had been sick this past month, throwing up nonstop. Me and Carlos had made shit official and no lie, I thought he would die when I told him I was pregnant. To my surprise, he was happy and made me promise I'd keep it, so I agreed.

38

I was praying for a girl so I could name her Cashmere, which was close to my best friend's name. Next month, we would find out the baby's sex, and Carlos was more excited than me.

Carlos was my boo from the flat line projects. He was, of course, an d-boy but he barred so much class. He had two kids but his baby mama had moved on and was now married so I didn't have the typical baby mama drama.

My ringing phone knocked me out my thoughts. I looked at the caller ID and it was Diane, me and Cash's other friend.

"Hello?"

"Hey, Malina," Diane chimed.

"What's da deal, boo?"

"I'm in town, I was tryna see what you were doing?"

"Girl, on my way to Nino's house. Blaze called me to come ASAP."

"Damn, is everything ok?"

"Shit, I don't know. I'm pulling up now."

39

"Well, I'm not hanging up until I make sure yall ok," Diane said, and we both laughed.

I walked into the home and damn near pissed on myself. Cash and her mother were sitting on the couch like they didn't have a care in the world.

"What the fuck!" I shouted and instantly began to cry.

"Hello, hello?" I almost forgot Diane was on the phone.

"Yeah, I'm here. Dee, you might wanna get over here, now."

"Say no more, I'm on my way," she hung up instantly.

I ran over to the two and hugged them both in a group hug. I guess they had gotten everything out because they were both laughing.

"You bitch!" I shouted and began playfully punching Cash in the chest.

"Ouch, hoe!" she shouted but kept laughing. "I ought to kick yo ass, Nina," Cash said with eyebrows raised, looking at my little round tummy.

Nino ran into the living room to see what was all the commotion then smiled when he realized what was going on.

"Nino, I'ma kick this hoe ass," I was still playfully punching her. Everybody laughed as we play fought.

When I stopped to catch my breath, I noticed a fine ass brother standing next to Nino. I knew I had no business looking but damn, he was fine.

"Damn, Nino, where you been hiding this skeez?" I wobbled over to the two and shook his hand. They both began to laugh right when Nino spoke up.

"Nina, this Bronx, my brother. Bro, this Nina, Cash's best friend."

"Wait! What the…" I looked over at Cash and this hoe dropped her head. "Oh my," I covered my mouth with my hand.

Bronx smiled and Nino didn't look too pleased.

"Cash is the man!" I thought to myself, smiling.

These niggas looked just alike. I'm talking from the same muscular built bodies to their long locks. The only difference was Bronx appeared a little older and his eyes were a bit lighter than Nino's.

"The Carter Boys, huh? Yall don't have another brother that look like yall, cause damn!" I said, causing the entire room to burst out into laughter.

"Shut your pregnant ass up, Nina, before I call Carlos," Blaze said, emerging from the back room.

We all laughed again.

Blaze and Carlos had become pretty cool. At first, Blaze was iffy about him, but then Carlos started copping work from him so he opened up a little.

I was so happy, I couldn't stop smiling. I had my crew back and now we could work together to get Que back, then we'd be back to one happy family. Life couldn't get any better.

Brooklyn Nino

After we sat around and talked, I had the chef hook us up a meal. Diane showed up, and of course, she cried, then laughed, and then cried again. A nigga was so happy right now that I actually departed from everyone and went to my room to say a prayer. I had my brother back in my life and not to mention, the love of my life was here in the flesh. I missed her ass like crazy.

I knew shit was about to get hectic in these streets because of what Bronx had explained to me about the Cartel. I didn't give a fuck, though, because our crew was made of one hundred percent killa's and we had the powerful Ms. Lopez back on the streets.

Ms. Lopez possessed so much power like Griselda Blanco around this bitch so I knew shit could get wild. I was happy to hear my brother killed Ricky's bitch ass. I'm mad I couldn't be the one to do it but it got handled and that was all that mattered.

Everybody had left, but before they did, we planned a cookout for the following day, at Ms. Lopez's house.

I tried to talk my brother into calling his wife but he felt right now wasn't the time so I didn't push him any further. He said he was staying at a hotel nearby but I told him he could stay with me until he was ready to go home to his family.

"Hey, bae," Cash said, walking into the room.

I quickly got up to help her through the door, I could tell she was in pain.

"You good, ma?"

"Yeah, I'm fine. It only hurts when the meds wear off, other than that, I'm ok, Brook," she smiled.

I helped her get in the bed, I could tell she had had a long ass day and the feelings were vice versa.

I pushed a loose piece of hair out her face and got lost in her big brown eyes. Cash was the most beautiful woman that ever walked this earth, to me. Just looking at her had my dick rock hard but I knew she was tired so I fell back. I still had questions that I needed truthful answers to, but that as well, I left alone until it was the right time to ask.

"I love you, Brooklyn Nino Carter."

"I love you more, Cash Nino Lopez," I said and made her smile widely.

"Man, ma, you just don't know. A nigga been sick without you."

"I could only imagine."

She shook her head and then rested it on my bare chest. Before I knew it, she was asleep and snoring lightly. I laid there in deep thought, kissing her numerously on the top of her head until I had finally dozed off.

Chapter 4

Cash

The Cookout...

When I opened my eyes, I rolled over to cuddle under Brook, but he was gone. Therefore, I got out of bed and headed into the restroom. Today, I would be doing everything on my own so yes, I would be dumping these damn crutches.

I went into the restroom to handle my hygiene, and then hopped in the shower. Today, I was going to get dressed because over this last week, I felt like a bum in Carter's oversized t-shirts.

When I stepped out the shower, I began looking through my closet I had in Brooklyn's home. Because it was nice and hot, I settled on a black, gray and red, "Kiss My Klass" halter dress, and my Gucci shoes that matched perfectly. I didn't know what I would do with my hair because it was all over the place. Fuck it, I was going to pop up to Nikki's house so she could hook me up. Brooklyn had told me he shut the shop down so I knew more than likely she was doing hair out of her salon at home.

Now that I was back, I'd be opening my club and barber shop but I wanted to wait until the cookout was over and done with. Business had to go on, so after today, I would be hitting up the ladies to let them know "Trap Gyrl" was back up and running.

I grabbed my Gucci Bag and headed downstairs to find Brooklyn. I searched the entire house and he was nowhere to be found. I grabbed the keys to his spider and made my way out the door, damn it felt good to be back.

When I pulled up to Nikki's, I couldn't call her because my phone was at home, in my purse, turned off from the night I didn't want to bothered with Brooklyn. I had just found out Brook and Carter, whose real name is Bronx, were brothers. Brook and I had a fall out so when I got home, I powered it off and headed to my swimming pool to relieve some tension. I swam a few laps and before I knew it, I was being snatched out of my pool and knocked

47

unconscious from the butt of a pistol. I was being held captive by my ex who the entire time I thought his name was Ricky. Come to find out, his real name was Al and he was the son of Big Al who had caused havoc in the streets before he was murdered by the hands of Brooklyn.

A knock at the driver window knocked me out my thoughts. Marvin, Nikki's husband, was standing there with a huge smile on his face. I opened the door and stepped out to greet him. He pulled me in for a hug, I then explained to him a little of what happened. He told me how Nikki had been distraught without me. He also informed me she was in her salon reading, so I walked into the home to surprise her.

"Hey, boo!" I shouted, causing Nikki to look from her book.

Her eyes grew as wide as saucers. She jumped up and ran over to me with tears streaming down her face.

"Oh my God, Cash! Oh my God," she said and her hands were shaking.

"Girl, I can't even cry no more," I caused us both to giggle.

After I let her get it all out, she walked me over to the hairstyling chair. I didn't even have to tell her why I had come because she was already running her fingers through my hair, shaking her head.

"Sit yo ass down, ma. This hair is a mess," she said and we both laughed.

After we were done with my hair, I told her about the cookout and she promised to come by. I also informed her that we would be opening the shop tomorrow and to call all the girls and invite them to the cookout. I would wait until the weekend to open up Juice. All I had to do was post one status on Facebook, and boom, both my businesses would be back popping.

Nikki handed me a hand mirror to examine my hair when we were finished. She had to give me a hard press and re-dyed my red highlights. She styled it with a middle part and left it long, flowing over my shoulders. I tucked one side behind my ear and I now felt back to myself. Ms. Muthafuckin Cash Lopez!

By the time I pulled up to now me and my mother's home, it was 2:00 in the afternoon so I knew people would be showing up soon. I headed straight upstairs to my room to retrieve my iPhone 6. When I powered it on, I had ninety-six text messages and forty-two missed calls.

I walked back downstairs in search of my mother. She wasn't in the living room so I went out to the yard and she was sitting on the bench, talking to Pedro. She motioned with her hand for me to come over. Since I had ditched the crutches, I walked slowly over to them and took a seat in the middle.

"Cash, mi amor, you know you almost gave me a heart attack," Pedro spoke with his heavy accent.

"Who are you telling, Pedro, when them niggas called Brooklyn's phone, you were in the background screaming like a girl," I said and we all laughed.

"Diva!" Diane and Nina were walking through the door.

I jumped up and hugged them both but making sure I rubbed Nina's belly.

Right on time, I thought to myself because I felt uneasy sitting alone with my mother and Pedro. I knew sooner or later, the subject of our empire would be brought up and right now was not the time. I knew now because my mother was home, she'd want me out the game and if it was left up to Pedro, I would have been out like yesterday. But fuck that, I had gotten so accustomed to the life, I'd die before I left. Yes, my mother could have her throne back but this Princess would still be in the game.

Slowly, everyone was pulling in one by one. Niya had finally surfaced and I could tell she was feeling some type of way because Blaze and Tiny were now a couple. Nikki and Marvin had shown up and even a few of my workers were in attendance.

Where the fuck is Brooklyn? I thought to myself right when… "Gutta!" I shouted.

He jumped out of Brook's arms and ran over to me. Oh my, God, I was so happy to see my puppy.

Brook stood there with a huge smile on his face. Carter emerged from inside, followed by his bimbo. I simply smirked and continued to play with Gutta. Carter walked over to us and pet Gutta on top of her head, I felt uneasy by the way Brook was frowning. I quickly walked away and went to mingle with my friends and associates.

After talking to my girls for a while, I went to find my mother because everybody was yelling "Where's the

51

food." I saw that the door was slightly open so I walked out to the front yard. My mother was standing out front with Esco. It looked like they were in a heated conversation and all my mother kept saying was, "it's not the time to tell her." Whatever the conversation was about, Esco looked pissed off.

"Tell me what?" I asked, walking up on the two puzzled. Esco had a weird look on his face and my mother nudged at his arm.

"Cash!" Esco yelled, extending his arms for a hug.

"Hey, Esco," I smiled. Whatever it was he wanted to tell me, it seemed as if my mom didn't want me to know so I left it alone, but I made a mental note to self to ask her about it later.

Brooklyn Nino

I spent all day shopping for the perfect ring. Right now was the perfect time to purpose to Cash because everybody important in our lives was in attendance. After pacing Cash's bedroom floor, I built up the courage I needed and headed downstairs to find her. When I reached the bottom of the stairs, I heard Cash and Bronx in the kitchen talking just above a whisper.

"I'm with your brother now, Carter, and I love him."

"I understand that, ma. Just tell me all those feeling you had for a nigga gone, though?"

I stood off to the side and neither of them even saw me standing there. The way Cash looked at him had me feeling some type of way. Therefore, I slid the ring into my pocket. Fuck that! I wasn't about to be made a fool so I would hold off on this engagement until I knew for sure that what they once shared was over.

Cash pushed past Bronx but I never heard her answer his question and that shit had me hot. I shook my head repeatedly. Seeing them two like that had a nigga hurt inside. Cash walked back outside and Bronx went back into the living room to join his lady friend.

When I walked outside, I tried my hardest not to look Cash's way. I walked straight up to Ms. Lopez to see if the food was ready. When I stole a glance at Cash, she looked guilty as a muthafucka and that really made me unsure about her feelings for this nigga.

"Ms. Lopez, the food ready?"

"Yes, son, let me go make your plate for you," she said, and I followed her into the kitchen.

After she made my plate, I went upstairs to eat and be left alone. I had so much shit running through my mind I didn't want to be bothered with anybody.

When I heard the door open, I sighed because I figured it was Cash but to my surprise, it was Blaze. I stood up to give him a pound and then he joined me on the bed.

"You know I'm not a mad scientist or nothing, but nigga, something is on your mind," Blaze said, pulling out an already rolled blunt.

"I'm good, why you say that?"

"Because for one, nigga, you up here looking like a lost soul. Two, everybody outside having a good time. Three, you just reunited with your woman who just yesterday you thought was dead and here it is you cooped up in the room."

He had me. I ran my hands down my face and looked at Blaze before speaking.

"Man, I don't know what's up with her, Blaze. The way she be looking at that nigga Bronx isn't sitting well with me. It's like I wanna believe nothing happened between them but it's hard because I know how much love Cash had for the nigga."

"Did you talk to her about it?"

"Honestly, nah, because I haven't had time with her alone."

"Well, I'll tell you like this, my nigga. Put yourself in her shoes. She fell in love with you, not knowing you and Bronx were brothers. Not to mention, she thought the nigga was dead. I know Cash wouldn't risk losing you because I can say that she's madly in love with your ugly ass," Blaze said and we both laughed.

I just prayed what he was saying was true. I never loved any woman like I love Cash, but one thing I wouldn't be doing is competing with my own fucking brother over some pussy.

***

When I finally made it home after the barbecue, I was tired as fuck and didn't want to do shit but shower. I quickly peeled out my clothes and hopped in. Since Cash was opening her shop back up tomorrow I was going to get my dreads re-twisted, so right now, I let the water run over my entire body. I then grabbed my shampoo and began washing my locks, it made it easier for Nikki when I came with my hair washed and ready.

When I opened my eyes, Cash was standing there with the most sympathetic look. I quickly turned my back to her, unfazed by her presence. I began rinsing the conditioner out my hair and when I turned back around she was fully naked. She climbed into the shower but didn't say one word. She began tracing my tattoo with her finger that read CASH big as day.

56

"When you get this?" she asked.

"When I thought you were…" She hushed me up with one finger then kissed me passionately.

I couldn't even put up a fight. I kissed her back like this would be our last kiss. Hell, with the life we were living, you never know. I lathered up the towel then began washing her body. When I was done, she did the same thing and we then stepped out to dry off.

The moment we got into the room, I laid her back on the bed and dove in, head first. I couldn't wait to kiss my pretty pussy. Not even five minutes our session, I had her legs shaking and on the verge of cumming. Ten minutes later, I knew she was having an orgasm because her legs shook uncontrollably and she screamed for me to stop. Because of her wombs, I slowly lifted her up off the bed and bent that ass over. I slid every last inch into her warm, wet pussy. Her shit was nice and tight just how I had left it. Maybe she didn't fuck that nigga.

"Damn, ma, yo shit tight," I said, going deeper. I knew I was hitting her with the death stroke because her mouth was open and she didn't utter one word.

"Oooh, shit, bae, oh my god, Brooklyn!"

57

"Stop running. Bring that ass here, ma," I grabbed her as she was trying to run. I plunged in and out her pussy, making sure she remembered this was the best dick she ever had.

After a good hour and half of sexing, we laid beside each other trying to catch our breath. She turned around to face me, so I took it as my cue dig deep. She looked me in my eyes, trying to read me. I damn near said fuck it but I had to know.

"Did you fuck him, Cash?"

She put her head down and at that moment, I didn't know what to think.

"No. No, Brooklyn. I swear I didn't, bae," she responded and she sounded so sincere.

"I believe you, ma," I spoke and kissed the top of her head.

"I was in a coma all this time, bae. I had only stayed with him for two days after I had woken up and the lady that was with him today was with us the entire time," she said and I sighed in relief. I just prayed she was telling me the truth. I pulled her close to me and kissed her passionately, there was nothing else to be said.

Chapter 5

Cash

Trap Gyrl was in full effect. All it took was one Facebook post and business was back booming. I missed my shop so much. It felt great to be sitting in my office and watching my cameras. All the girls were excited to see me and to my surprise, even Monique had shown up acting like she missed me.

"Surprise, bitch," was the look on my face when she walked into the shop. I was looking good and feeling great, not even Mo thot ass could ruin it.

All the ladies took their positions at their stations and patiently waited for their clients. I got up and walked back into the shop so I could mingle with everyone. A familiar face walked in and my blood began to boil. It was my first grand opening, and I was already about to whoop some ass.

"Bitch, what the fuck you doing in my shit?" I barked at Tiffany.

The bitch had the nerve to smirk at me, but when I ran up in her face, her smirk was turned into fear.

Tiffany was one of Brook's little groupies. I didn't know if she knew I owned the place or was she being funny, but I was for sure about to give this hoe a rude awakening. I cold cocked the hoe right between the eyes. She fell to the floor, holding her forehead as blood began to fall down her nose. Before I knew it, two of my workers shoved me out the way and started stomping her out. Out of nowhere, Brooklyn and Carter pulled the girls off Tiffany. When Brook noticed who it was, he went ballistic.

"Yo, why the fuck is you even here?" he asked, but the bitch was crying so hard, she couldn't even speak. He shoved her out the door and I followed right behind them, making sure the bitch didn't get a chance to say shit to my man.

"Gone, Tiff! Why the fuck you up here, anyway?"

"I didn't know, I'm sorry, I really didn't know!" she cried, looking from me to Brook.

I didn't have any sympathy for the bitch so I stood with my arms folded over my chest.

"Just get the fuck on before I shoot yo' shit up," I barked at her and she did just that.

When Brook tried to grab my arm, I pulled back. It was his fault I had to go through this shit. Had he known how to keep his dick in his pants, none of this would have transpired.

I stormed back into the shop and headed straight to my office. I retrieved the fifth of Hennessy I had in my cabinet and poured me a drink to calm my nerves.

"Don't let this fuck your day up," I thought to myself.

I got up to go apologies to my staff and clients. It had only been 48 hours since I'd been home and already, I had to go upside of one of Brooklyn's bitches head.

"Cash Lopez," an officer came through the door.

I looked at him and knew it had to be the bullshit with Tiffany. "Yes, officer?"

"So, you are Cash?"

"Yes," I spoke and put my head down.

Nikki ran over and locked the door, now I was really puzzled.

"What the fuck is going on?" I thought to myself.

He made me turn around and was ready to cuff me.

"What am I being arrested for, sir?" I kept asking, but not once did he respond, which was making me annoyed.

I turned to see what was taking so long, the cop was naked, only wearing a G-string. His hard rock body looked damn good and his sexy smile was enough to make any woman melt. I looked around the shop and just that fast, the ladies had their money out. I scanned the room for Brook and Carter and they appeared to be in my office.

Tyrese "Signs of Love Making" came blasting through the speakers. A mischievous grin crept across my face. These bitches set me up! Nikki then pulled up a chair for me to sit down and then ran to unlock the door for Nina and Diane. The moment Nina walked in, she handed me a duffle bag full of $10 bills and she began making it rain on the both of us. Diane was shouting at the top of her lungs

63

and smacking the dancer on his ass as she threw money at his backside. The ladies were going wild and I knew this would be a day to remember.

Brooklyn Nino

"Hello?"

"Yo, Bronx, you ready?"

"Yeah, you outside?"

"I'm pulling up in about five minutes."

"A'ight, bet," I hung up with my brother.

Today was a big day for him. I was going to take him to see his wife and kids. This shit was about to be crazy. I just prayed Lydia wouldn't kill us both. More than likely, she would assume I knew this entire time he was alive, but shit, I was just as much in the loop as her.

I pulled up to the hotel Bronx was staying at and he was already outside waiting. He hopped in and gave me a pound and we drove off, heading to the freeway.

"You nervous?" I asked because he was a little too quiet.

"Hell yeah, man. Lydia gone kill a nigga."

"Just make sure you tell her I didn't know shit," I said, causing us both to laugh.

"Man, I know Bri Bri going to be happy to see a nigga. I left when she was young, but I'm sure she remembers me because I couldn't even shit in peace without that girl on me."

We both laughed again.

"I know Lydia is going to want me home but I can't stay there yet, Nino. These muthafuckas gonna come sooner or later and I don't wanna bring no harm to my family."

"I feel you, man. Well, you could come stay at my crib, I keep telling you that."

"I know, I'm going to come soon as I send this bitch back on a plane," Bronx said, referring to his lady friend that had accompanied him to the US.

When I looked over at him, I could tell he had a lot on his mind. I wanted to holla at him about Cash, but I left it alone because he was already about to encounter the raft of Lydia.

When we pulled up, Lydia's ride was parked out front and there was a Porsche Panamera parked beside it. Bronx's face was screwed up, I knew he was just as curious as me. We dead the engine and hopped out at the same time.

When we got to the door, the entire house looked as if nobody was home. Bronx knocked twice. We waited for someone to answer. Growing impatient, I was about to go knock on the back door right when the door came opening slowly. A man opened the door with no shirt on and had the nerve to ask, "Who were we looking for?"

"Who the fuck is you, nigga?"

"Nigga, you at my house," the guy shouted.

"Your house? Where the fuck Lydia at?" Bronx pushed past and I followed behind him. It was about to go down and I just prayed we didn't have to body this nigga.

"Who are you?" the man asked again.

66

"Nigga, who the fuck are you, answering my wife's door?"

"Your wife?" the guy asked puzzled.

Before I knew it, Bronx stole one to his jaw and my brotherly instinct kicked in and we began stomping the nigga out.

"Oh my God! Stop! Please! Bronx! Brook! Please!" Lydia came down the stairs screaming. Her face had a million tears and I could tell she was stunned to see her husband's face.

I finally got Bronx to stop pouncing on ol boy. That nigga was in a rage, he was breathing hard and he had the look of the Devil.

"What the fuck is going on?" Lydia began to sob.

"Who the fuck is this nigga, Lydia?"

"What the fuck you mean, Bronx? You barge into my home and start questioning me? Nigga, you supposed to be dead. Oh my God, you're supposed to be dead!" she shouted, shoving Bronx in the chest.

He looked from Lydia to the guy still laying on the floor, back to Lydia. Right when…

"Daddy!" Brianna came running down the stairs, followed by Brittany. They jumped into his arms and Brittany began to cry. Britt was old enough to understand what was going on, however, Bri was too young to know her pops had basically rose from the dead.

"Yall put yall shoes on, yall going with me," Bronx said, and the kids ran off to do as told.

"Where are you taking my kids?"

"Man, get the fuck out my face, Lydia."

"Nigga, you ain't taking my fucking kids!"

"Look, just handle your little boyfriend. I'm taking my kids with me and I'll bring them back in a few days," and just like that, he walked out, leaving his wife with tears and thoughts.

Damn! was all I could say, but I followed suit.

I hated to have left Lydia like that, but I could only imagine how my brother felt. It wasn't the fact that Lydia had moved on, but damn, she had a nigga laying up in the crib my brother bought and not to mention, around his kids. I wanted to holla at him but I knew right now wouldn't be a great time so I left it alone until he cooled down.

***

I woke up the next morning feeling like shit. I had stayed up with Bronx all night, throwing back shots of Henny. Bronx and the kids came to stay over at the house with me and Cash. He sent his lady friend back home on his private jet as soon as we got back from Lydia's. I knew my brother like the back of my hand, he was more hot-headed than me so I knew Lydia's male companion wouldn't be breathing past the next seventy-two hours. If Lydia knew I like I knew, she would have sent ol boy away for good. Before Bronx had gone away, he and Lydia had just patched up their relationship. They were split up for almost a year so more than likely that's when he and Cash had their little fling.

After I handled my hygiene, I went downstairs to find my baby. She was sitting on the couch talking to my sister Breela, and Bri Bri was standing behind her playing in her hair. I don't know why but I kind of felt jealous because Bri was Carter's, which would make Cash her long lost stepmother. I quickly shook off the thought and joined them on the couch.

"Hey, drunky," Cash greeted me, laughing.

"Yeah, you were wasted last night, bro," my little sister added her two cents.

"Shut your big head ass up, Breela," I playfully hit her upside her head.

Breela was visiting from college. She had two more years before finishing up her master's, which explained why she hadn't been around. She left off to school after Bronx's fake ass funeral. I had missed it because I was locked up serving a violation. I had to hear from the punk ass deputies that my brother had gotten murdered. Because I was on high-risk parole, they felt it wouldn't have been a good idea to let me attend the funeral.

He had mentioned Cash to me before I went to jail but I was so heavy in the streets, I never got a chance to meet her. After the death of Bronx, I was released a few months later, that's when the infamous Cash name began to surface.

70

"Uncle Brook, can we go swimming?" Bri Bri asked me, knocking me out my chain of thoughts.

"Yeah, Bri, tell aunty Cash to go put yo swimsuit on, baby."

"Yayyy!" Bri yelled and Cashed lifted up to go help her.

Cash's eyes lit up like a seven-year-old child at just the mention of swimming. That shit was too funny. Cash loved swimming, no matter the weather, that girl would be out in the rain in the pool. I had on some basketball shorts so I was just fine.

I headed outside to wait for the girls and my phone rung, which was great because I almost forgot I had it in my pocket and I was about to jump straight into 12 feet.

"Hello?"

"Hello? Brooklyn?"

"Yeah, who is this?"

"I was just calling to say I'm sorry about the other day. I swear I didn't know that was your girl shop," Tiffany cried into the phone.

"How the fuck you get my number?" I asked. Fuck everything she was talking about. I just wanted to know how this bitch got my line.

"I got it from Breela."

"Yeah, aight… well, don't trip, just stay away from there."

"Ok," she sniffled and I immediately hung up.

"Breela!" I called for my sister before Cash came down.

After a few moments, she came from out the house with a puzzled look.

"You gave that bitch Tiffany my number?"

"Yeah, she said she had talked to you, and…"

I cut her off before she could finish.

"Man, that hoe is a lie. Don't ever give my number to nobody without hollering at me first."

"Ok," she replied.

"Is everything ok?" Cash asked.

I wondered how long she had been standing there. I wasn't tripping or nothing, I just didn't want her jumping to conclusions.

"Yeah, everything straight, ma," I said, pulling Cash by her bikini bottoms.

She was blushing so hard.

I had to hurry and jump in the water because a nigga dick was rock hard watching her in that little ass two piece. Cash jumped in behind me, followed by Breela. Bri Bri went in two feet and slowly got in with her floaty around her. I swam under the water right up to Cash. She was so busy playing with Breela, she didn't even see me coming until I bit her on the monkey from under the water. She wrapped her legs around my neck before I could make it from under the water so I swam with her in my arms to twelve feet.

"You betta be lucky the kids in here or you'll be coming out this shit," I told her, tugging at her bottoms.

She giggled then grabbed my dick. "You nasty," she said and splashed me with water, then she swam off in a hurry. Cash knew how to swim like a muthafucka but when I caught her ass, it was on.

Chapter 6

Cash

"Cash Lopez!" After forty-five minutes of waiting, my name was finally called.

I got up to retrieve my pass and then headed down the long hallway. When I finally reached the window, my heart fell into the pit of my stomach. His eyes fell onto me and he looked so shocked to see me. We locked eyes for what seemed like an eternity, then I finally sat down and picked up the phone.

Without a word, we stared at each other until I began to fidget. Slowly, a smile crept across his face and that dimple he showed made me smile widely.

"Wifey!" he shouted, and I couldn't stop smiling.

"Hey, Que," I finally spoke.

74

"Damn, ma, you the last person I thought I'd see," he stared at me, not believing it was me.

"Yes, it's me in the flesh."

"How? What the…" he said, stumbling over his words. He just shook his head, and then dropped the phone along with his head.

I gave him some time to grasp what was going on and after a few minutes, I called his name while tapping on the glass window, "Que."

When he looked back up at me, he had a single tear flowing from his left eye. At that moment, I couldn't even hold it back anymore. My tears came pouring down while we looked each other deeply in the eyes.

"I'm not even gonna ask, ma," he shook his head.

"Yeah, it's a long story."

"Just tell me where you been, though?"

"Carter rescued me from Ricky."

"Carter?" Que asked, puzzled.

"Yes, Carter. He wasn't dead all this time, Que," again, I began to cry again.

Que had this funny look on his face at the mention Carter's name, but I brushed it off and continued my story.

"He had been following me all this time. He's the reason I'm alive today. When I woke up, he informed me that I was in a coma for three weeks."

"This shit crazy," Que said, shaking his head.

"Imagine how I feel."

"Did you fuck that nigga, Cash?" he asked, causing me to laugh. Que had always been jealous of any nigga so I knew sooner or later that question would come up.

"No, Que. I'm with his brother now. Everything me and Carter had is over with."

"So, what's up, ma, how you feeling?" he asked, changing the subject.

"I'm great. I'll be even better when you get out of here."

"I know, man. I'm waiting to go to court so I could try and get a bond."

76

"My mother's home," I said, cheerfully.

"I know. How is she doing?"

"She's fine. She's just chilling for now but you know her, she'll be right back at doing what she do."

We both laughed.

"Aye, ma, listen up, tho. Ol boy can't babysit my baby anymore. You gotta fire his ass. My baby mama got him tucked away so holla at Marcus and Diane," Que said, speaking in codes. I knew exactly what he was talking about.

"Ok, I got you," I nodded and dead that subject.

"So when are you gone open up the shop and shit?"

"I opened the shop, I'll be opening the club this weekend."

"That's what's up," he nodded his head.

"I miss you so much."

"I miss you too, wifey. A nigga gone be back on them streets, watch. But too bad you all in love, tho, I can't get no more of my pussy," he said and we both laughed.

"Boy, you still crazy."

"Nah, I'm just fucking with you. Nino my nigga, man."

I couldn't help but smile because once upon a time, Que wanted Brook's head. I'm glad that they can finally get along because it was more peaceful without the two gunning for each other.

"So why haven't you called?"

"Shit, honestly, I just been chilling, waiting to go to court. Aye, I gotta go, ma. Find out if Nino ever took that money to Keisha for me too, ma."

Now I was puzzled because Brook never mentioned about his dealings with Keisha.

"Ok. I love you."

"I Love you too. And, I'ma call you in a few days, ok?"

"Ok," I shook my head right when the guard came to get him.

He smiled, causing me to smile back. He hit me with that side shot so I could see that dimple. I laughed

78

because he knew exactly what he was doing. I walked down the hall along with Que and the guard until he was escorted through a door.

The moment I got into the car, I called Blaze first. I then called Diane, and next, Marcus. It was time to get back in these streets and make shit happen for Que. I called a mandatory meeting at the safe house and then jumped on the highway straight there. The ringing of my phone knocked me out my thoughts. My Nicki Minaj and Meek Mill ringtone let me know it was Brook so I answered through my Bluetooth car speakers.

"Hey, bae."

"What's up, Lil mama. How did the visit go?"

"It was cool. I'm actually on my way to the safe house for a meeting."

"Oh, so you weren't gon call me?"

"It ain't like that, bae. I was just moving too fast. Meet me there, tho."

"Aight, I'll be there in a sec."

"Ok, love you."

"Love you more, ma."

When I pulled up, just like I suspected, Blaze was already here along with his new Bonnie, Tiny, and Marcus. When I walked in, Tiny was on his lap and Marcus was doing what he does best, on the computer. I took my seat at the head of the table and we waited for Brook and Diane. I looked over at the space across from me where Que once sat and it felt weird not having him here.

After about fifteen more minutes, Diane strutted in like the Diva she was, with a briefcase in hand and took her seat. Shortly after, Brook walked in followed by Bronx, I couldn't help but smile at the two. Once everybody was seated and I had their undivided attention, I began to speak.

"I went to visit Que today," I said, looking around the room. "He was speaking in codes but he basically said the police were hiding Mike and we need him dead, ASAP. Diane, what you got for us?"

"Well, Que's case is looking good, thanks to Ms. Lopez. The drugs were confiscated from the evidence room. The only evidence they have is Mike. Also, I have a friend that's a judge, she wants one million and she would basically destroy Mike's first statement and the audio of him tapping the transaction between him and Que. The only thing incriminating is Mike showing up to court. The police are doing a great job at hiding him because they know he's all they have. At first, they were after you, Cash, but again thanks to Ms. Lopez, the Chief was paid off and now you're no longer a subject. The Chief is the one that feels it won't be a good idea to get Que off because it would raise suspicion, however, he did say he would try his best," Diane spoke and everybody nodded their heads.

"Ok, we'll pay the million dollars. Come by the house first thing tomorrow, Diane, I'll have that ready for you. Marcus, have you been able to locate anything on Mike?" I asked, looking over at Marcus as he punched the keys on his laptop.

"I had a location on him but unfortunately, the un-dirty cops moved him. I'm more than sure that he's living under the roof of one of the cops or he's in another state. I've searched the states and federal database, and I'm having hell locating him. At first, he was being housed in Louisiana with some relatives but me trying to locate him, tipped them off so they moved him. Because this is federal, they have access to more personal data, so that's the problem I'm having now. If I keep trying to search him in my system, it would alarm them and within 24 hours, they'll more than likely move him again," Marcus said, then began looking at his screen.

Right when I was about to speak, the door flew open and my mother came sashaying her ass in.

"Hey, ma?" I said and she walked up to me, planting a kiss on my cheek.

"I came to give you this," she handed me a piece of paper with an out of state address.

"What's this?" I asked, puzzled.

"That's what you need, right? It's the address to where Mike is being hidden," she said and walked right back out the door.

I shook my head repeatedly and couldn't help but chuckle.

"Ms. Lopez is something else," Blaze said, causing the entire room to laugh.

I then looked at Tiny, forgetting she was in the room until her I heard her giggle.

"Tiny, so how you feel about everything because we can't be having…"

Before I could finish, she spoke up. "Honestly, Cash, I'm rolling with you like I've been doing since day one. Mike is bitch ass a snitch. baby daddy or not, he gotta go. He hasn't been giving two fucks about me or my kids so fuck the nigga. Plus, I'm with Blaze now, so I'm going to ride with him to the wheels fall off," Tiny spoke and Blaze started smiling from ear to ear.

"Tiny, what you do to this nigga?" Brook said, and we all laughed.

Marcus was laughing so hard, we all looked in his direction.

"What's so funny, nigga? Blaze playfully said to Marcus.

"Well, actually you are, Blaze. I've been doing business with you guys since Ms. Lopez was out and not once had I seen you with a woman until the day you and Ms. Tiny were at the trap house getting it on," Marcus said, and we really started to laugh.

"Nigga, how you know about that?" Blaze asked, laughing. He then looked at me because I'm the one that caught they ass.

"Um, easy. Remember, I'm the one that controls all the cameras in each trap house," Marcus said and we all laughed again.

We were amused by Marcus because he never spoke unless it was about an assignment. Marcus was geeky as hell and very good at what he did. It was actually shocking that he was involved with us because he could have worked for any major company in the world. More than likely, he stayed not only because of loyalty to my mother but we paid him double of what he would make anywhere else.

The look Carter was giving me was making me feel weird. I had looked up and caught him several of times. I was silently praying he would stop before Brook took notice and flipped out. I walked over to Brook and took a seat on his lap. Out the corner of my eyes, I could see Carter getting annoyed but I kept straight and focused my attention on Brooklyn.

Chapter 7

Que

I can't believe this shit! I cursed myself over and over. This bitch ass nigga Carter wasn't dead and I knew it was only a matter of time he would tell I was the one that shot him. He wasn't my only problem, though. Since he was still alive, I knew that the Cartel would come after me. I just prayed they wouldn't harm Cash behind my foolish acts.

"Looks like you have a lot on your mind?" Deputy Williams asked with a smirk. I really didn't feel like being bothered but fuck it, the only way to relieve stress was some good pussy.

"Hell yeah, ma. Won't you come up in here and get my mind right," I flirted back.

She looked up the tier a few times, making sure the coast was clear, then slid into my cell quietly. As soon as she walked in, she pulled her uniform pants down, causing my dick to rock up. I bent her thick ass over my bunk and pushed my dick right up in her fat pussy. I don't know what was up with her husband at home but that nigga wasn't hitting it right because every time she slid into my cell, her pussy was dripping wet.

From the first day I stepped foot in this muthafucka, Deputy Williams was on a nigga. What was crazy was every nigga in the jailhouse wanted her fine ass, but she wouldn't give them niggas the time of day. One day, she came into my cell and moved my bunkie out. The next day, she called herself raiding my shit, talking about she heard I had a burner. I pinned that ass up on the wall and kissed her like we were starring in a Hollywood movie. She quickly ran out my cell noid but the bitch wasn't to noid because the next day in the wee hours of the night, I woke up to her with her lips round my dick. I was having a dream about Cash already so soon as I felt her warm lips, I just knew I was having a wet dream. When my eyes flung open, I looked into the eyes of Deputy Williams freaky ass. She sucked me up until I came in her mouth and quickly ran out to her booth. Every chance I got since that day, I was hitting that shit. And just like now, I had her talking in tongues.

"Shit, Que!" she shouted as I pumped in and out her pussy, viciously.

"You like this thug dick, huh?"

"Yes, I love it, oh my God, I love it."

"You gone be a good pig and swallow it, right?"

"Yes… oh, yes. Just let me know…."

Before she could finish, I spun her ass around and she immediately took her position. She started sucking me off until every ounce of cum I had in me was down her throat. I leaned up against the wall, trying to catch my breath and she quickly pulled her pants up and tucked her shirt back in.

"So who was that, that came to visit you today, Quintin?" she said, calling me by my government.

"That was Cash, ma," I replied and she quickly caught an attitude.

"Come here, baby girl, stopping pouting," I pulled her into my arms. "You ain't got shit to worry about. Cash is married now and me and her dude cool, aight?"

"Ok," she shook her head with the saddest puppy dog eyes.

"Now, gone before you get caught," I said and patted her on her ass.

No lie, I was feeling the shit out of Deputy Williams. Not only was she sexy as fuck, but she saw something in a nigga that she didn't see in any other inmate. It's been plenty times she asked if I needed something like food, a cell phone or even tobacco, but I'd always say no and that's what made me really like her. A nigga was rolling in dough so I didn't need the petty cash or extra drama that came with it. I, for damn sure, didn't plan on being here that long.

I laid up on my bunk and couldn't get Cash's sexy ass off my mind. No matter how close me and Nino got, she would always have that place in my heart that no other bitch would have. I knew it was only a matter of time before she handled Mike for me so for now, I would chill until I was a free man.

***

A few days had gone by, and I pretty much just chilled. I went out to the tier to use the phone. I dialed my

88

nigga Young's number and prayed he answered because I needed to check my traps. I knew Cash and Ms. Lopez had shit on lock on the streets but I needed to make sure my shit was still intact. After waiting for about four rings, he finally answered and quickly hit five to accept the call.

"Yo?"

"What's good, Youngin?"

"Shit, what's da deal, Que?"

"Shit, just checking in. How shit looking out there?"

"Shit, everything straight. Ms. Lopez handled yo shit and I gave her your dough, too."

"Oh ok, good looking."

"Aye, my nigga, I got something to tell you," Young said, sounding unsure if he wanted to say whatever was bothering him.

"Holla at me, nigga."

"Keisha came through on some weird shit."

"Weird like what?"

89

"Ol girl playing with her nose, man."

I got quiet. This nigga just dropped a bombshell on me, all I could do was shake my head.

"Is that right?"

"Yeah, man. She begged me not to tell you but you know I had to tell you, man."

"Yeah, good looking. Aye, if that bitch comes back through there, run her ass up out of there, you hear me?"

"Yep, I got you."

"And, make sure you tell them other niggas that too. If I find out a nigga served my BM, I'm bodying shit and you already know."

"I already know, man."

"Well, look, nigga, I gotta go. Hold shift down for me, Young."

"You know I am, my nigga."

"A'ight, one."

"One…"

I slammed the phone down and headed back to my cell. I was mad as a muthafucka, no lie. I couldn't wait to get home, kick this hoe out my house, and take my fucking daughter. This bitch had everything in the world and she rather get high. Now it all came back to me. She always complained about needing money. I made sure Blaze paid the bills and not to mention, I left the bitch forty gee's, I guess that wasn't enough.

"Damn, how much this bitch sniffing?" I thought to myself right when Deputy Williams walked up to my cell.

"What bitch got you mad now, Quintin?" she snapped, making the situation worst.

"Not now, ma!" I barked at her.

She just looked at me like she was ready to cry but honestly, I didn't give two fucks. I'd deal with her later. She then reached into her pockets and pulled out a piece of paper and tossed it on my floor and stormed off. At first, I was hesitant about picking it up but What the hell, I thought and reached over.

My eyes grew wide the more I read, this shit had to be a joke. I furiously balled up the paper and threw that shit back on the ground. I shook my head so much; I knew this muthafucka would eventually fall off. This bitch Pregnant!

Brooklyn Nino

Cash and I scrambled around our room getting dressed. Tonight was the reopening of "Juice" and we were running behind schedule. Her ass was prancing around in the mirror and if she kept it up, I was going to bend that ass over and plunge up in her. She was looking sexy as hell in her Valentino Embellished gown. The split that went all the way up to her thigh had my dick hard as penitentiary steel. Nikki had whipped her hair up nice and my baby was looking like she was stepping into Beyonce's bday party. I was looking GQ my damn self in my Balmain Jeans, an Ermenegildo Zegna Blazer, and my Giuseppe Zanotti high top sneakers that exhilarated my look. My dreads were freshly twisted and I was iced out the game. I had to match Lil Mama's fly because tonight, I was gonna do the unthinkable.

"Come on, ma. We're running late."

"I'm coming, bae, I'm coming," she said, putting on her lip gloss.

I walked to the closet and grabbed both my burners and tucked them both on each side of my waist. I pulled Dolly out the closet and bent down to strap her onto Cash's ankle just how she liked. When she was finally finished, we headed out the door and the Maybach was waiting for us right at the door.

I greeted James my driver then hopped in, followed by Cash. She immediately grabbed the remote I just prayed she didn't play Nikki and Meek. To my surprise, she switched the cd and turned up Jeremih's "Impatient" ft. Ty Dolla. I was fine with that because this was my shit. She then poured us a glass of D'usse Cognac as James pulled out of the driveway heading for the highway.

***

When we pulled up to Juice, the outside crowd went crazy. The people that knew Cash were happy as hell to see her and that shit made a nigga feel good. When we stepped inside, the club DJ was bumping "Panda," so the club was beyond turnt up. Looking around at how packed the place was ensured me my lady was "That Bitch," hands down. She posted this shit on Facebook one time and this muthafucka was jumping like it hadn't been closed a whole month and a half.

Cash and I made our way through the crowd and headed to our normal VIP section. The whole crew was already here, even Nina's pregnant ass along with Carlos.

Nobody knew but me, Ms. Lopez and the DJ that I was going to propose tonight, so everybody was pretty much clueless. Everything would take place at 1 am sharp and right now, it was only 11:16 so for now, I would max back with my boys.

I caught Cash right before she walked off. I pulled her close to me and whispered in her ear.

"You look beautiful tonight, ma."

"Awww, thank you, bae," she said, kissing me on each cheek.

She was nestled up under my arm when Quan walked up to greet her. She began to step away from me, but not before I spoke.

"Get that nigga bodied tonight if you want to, lil mama," I said, letting go of her hand.

95

She patted my arm and smiled for reassurance that she wasn't on no bullshit so I fell back and let her do her.

See, I wasn't no hater type nigga but the night Cash and I hooked up, she was on a date with this nigga Quan. Cash's ass wasn't no angel but I had to trust her, especially after what I would being doing tonight. I let her go say hi to the nigga but I made sure to pay close attention to the two because I knew he wanted her in the worse way. Quan wasn't really a threat. True, he was a decent guy and getting major money but the nigga wasn't me… Straight up!

I walked over to my nigga Kellz and made small talk about our traps. Marie thirsty ass came out of nowhere and this shit was like Deja Vu.

"What's up, Nino?"

"What's the deal, Marie?"

"You!" she shot at me, but I brushed that shit off.

"Man, gone somewhere before my girl comes over here and bust you upside your fucking head, ma," I turned my back on her.

"It looks like your girl occupied to me," she smirked before walking off.

96

I wasn't even about to let that thot get to me so I brushed that off to. However, I did sneak a peek over at Cash and Quan, and yeah, they had been doing a little too much conversing for me.

"Say bye to your little friend," I whispered in her ear but loud enough for him to hear me. I mugged him at the same time and waited for him to say one slick thing.

"Nino, what's up, my nigga?" he said, extending his hand for a shake.

I shook his hand and hit him with a head nod, but that shit was fake as fuck. Quan and I used to be cool until he found out I wifed Cash. True, he was fucking with her, but she was single so when I did wife her, she now belonged to me.

I guess Cash felt the tension because she told him, "Nice seeing you" and walked off while pulling at my blazer to follow her.

"Bae, you crazy. You know damn well I would never disrespect you, and especially for Quan."

"I don't give a fuck about all that, ma. I don't want the nigga smiling all up in your face. I was tryna be cool and let you say hi, but you took that and ran with it."

"Oh my God, boy!" she shouted and walked off to talk to her girls. I didn't give two fucks about all that. My bitch wasn't about to be entertaining another nigga, especially a nigga she fucked before.

I walked over to Blaze and he was laughing quietly.

"What, nigga?" I asked, smiling because I knew what he was thinking.

"Yo, don't make me start calling you, Que Jr.," he said and we all started laughing.

He wasn't lying, though, because Que was so in love with Cash, a nigga couldn't even ask her for the time. That boy gave me hell when me and Cash first started dating. Her ass didn't tell me she was fucking on him, though, because if I had known, I wouldn't have stepped on my nigga Que's toes.

Cash a cold piece of work and she know it too, I thought to myself while shaking my head.

She was standing over to the side with her girls. I stood back and admired everything about her. She was rocking a 28,000-dollar dress, looking like a fucking princess, but had a 9-milli tucked in her ankle. That was the sexist shit in the world to me.

I kept checking my phone for the time and it seemed as if time was moving fast than a muthafucka. I swigged the bottle I was holding as much as I could because a nigga was nervous than a muthafucka. I looked from her to my brother with a million things running through my mind. I just prayed to God I wasn't about to make a mistake. I quickly shook off the thoughts and prepared myself for what I was about to do, I just hoped I didn't regret it.

Chapter 8

Cash

Standing across the room with lustful eyes, I examined Brook closely. He looked so fucking good tonight, I was ready to pull him into the bathroom and let him bend me over the sink. I had to admit, the little jealous stunt he pulled with Quan kind of turned me on. Brook was tripping in a major way but little did he know, Quan wasn't even worth me losing him. I loved Brooklyn to death and being nearly killed made me realize it that much more.

"Damn, bitch, yall going home together," Niya said, laughing.

I looked over at her, caught red handed, and I couldn't help but blush.

"She over here mind fucking the poor guy," Diane said and again, we all laughed.

"He sooo bomb, y'all," I smiled from ear to ear.

The music stopped and you could hear the voices throughout the entire club. I walked over to the ledge to look down into the crowd. I had to make sure wasn't shit going on and especially because this was my first night reopening. To my surprise, nothing seemed to be happening, so I figured the DJ was having problems with his equipment.

A single spot light came on and pointed directly onto me. I looked at DJ Bounce with a curious look on my face. He smiled and shook his arms as if he didn't know what was going on. When I turned around, Brooklyn was on one knee, he was holding what appeared to be at least 15 karats of diamonds. The ring was breathtaking. I looked into Brooklyn's pleading eyes as he proudly said the words, "will you marry me?" Now yall know I'm an emotional thug so of course, I began to cry.

"Yes, Brooklyn, yes!" I shouted as if sooner or later, he would change his mind.

He slid the ring onto my finger, stood up, and gave the DJ a thumbs up.

Bounce shouted over the mic. "She said yes, yall!"

The entire club went crazy!

The DJ then yelled into the mic, "Congrats, Nino, and Cash," then he played the perfect song that described me and Brooklyn's relationship.

Who wants that perfect love story, anyway?

Cliché, cliché.

Cliché, cliché.

Who wants that hero love that saves the day?

Cliché, cliché

Cliché, cliché.

As soon as Jay Z's part came on, Brooklyn pulled me close to him and began kissing me. Everything was so perfect.

"I love you, Cash Carter," he said and kissed me on top of my head.

"I love you more, Brooklyn Nino Carter," I said while looking him square dead in his eyes.

We cuddled up pretty much during the entire song until my girls came and stole me away.

"Oh my God, ma. Congratulations!" Nina ol pregnant, emotional ass was smiling and crying at the same.

"Thank you, ma," I began to cry with her.

The rest of the girls ran up to me and began hugging me. When I looked over at Brooklyn, the guys had him in the middle of their circle, popping bottle after bottle. Bronx seemed pretty excited or at least he pretended to be.

I walked over to my now fiancé and snuggled up under his arm. I was good and drunk by this time, therefore, it was time to fuck like we were trying to go half on a baby. My phone alerted me, letting me know I had a text. When I looked down, I couldn't help but smile.

Mommy: Congratulations, my child.

Me: Aww, thank you, Mommy. And what are you doing woke at this time a night?

Mommy: Getting my groove back. Now be safe and call me tomorrow.

Me: LOL, omg! Ok, Love you.

Mommy: Love you too, baby.

Right before the club would be closing, Brook and I left so we could beat the crowd and began our newlywed sexcapades. The moment we got into the car, he shut the window inside to divide us from the driver. He then slid his hands under my dress and pulled down my red lace thong. He turned me around so he could unzip the back of my dress. I was now asshole naked, in only my heels.

He began to undress and when he was fully naked, he pushed me back, threw my legs over his shoulders, and entered me slowly. My pussy was dripping wet. I instantly began to moan loudly, not giving two fucks who heard us. Brook was hitting me with nice long strokes. I don't know if it was the liquor or not, but it felt like the best sex in the world and at this moment, I didn't want this feeling to ever end.

Bronx Carter

The whole episode last night with Brooklyn and Cash made me realize I needed to take my ass home and patch shit up with Lydia. I prayed when I got home her little friend would be gone, and if not, I made up my mind to just let them be. I ain't going to lie, my first instinct said body the nigga but listening to my brother's lecture made me understand why I should just leave shit alone. I had been gone three years, away from her and my kids, so I understand she had to move on, eventually.

The day I dropped my kids off, I couldn't even face her so I let them out at the door and the minute I saw the door open, I sped off without a word. I hated to do her like but I wasn't ready to face her and I damn sure didn't want to see another nigga in my house.

By the time I reached the house, I parked and sat there for what seemed like forever. When I built up enough courage, I made my way to the door and patiently waited for her to open. When she finally opened the door, we just stared at each other without a word. Damn! She was looking good as a muthafucka like she knew I would be coming.

"Sup, ma?" I spoke and let myself in.

She didn't say one word, she just closed the door and took a seat on the cream leather sofa. I looked around my once old home and it looked nice like she had done some major decorating. I was surprised to see there were pictures of me, her, and kids hanging around the entire home. Lydia sat there quietly as if she was waiting for me to explain myself. I could tell she was a bit nervous by the way she was jittering in her seat. I took a seat across from her on the love seat and braced myself for the conversation that was about to take place.

"Look, ma, I apologize about what I did to your little boyfriend," I spoke and she just looked at me with the saddest eyes. "Is he here now?" I asked because if he was, I was going to leave in peace and leave the whole situation alone.

"No, he hasn't been here since that day," she said and put her head down.

"I know you probably upset with a nigga, but I did what I did to protect the family."

"But three years, Bronx? Three fucking years?" she began to cry.

"Look, ma. You know how much I keep you out my street life, the less you know, the less you could tell. I'ma give it to you the best way I could. A major Cartel is after me over some drugs. When I was heavy in the streets, my crew made a move and we took three hundred kilos from them. I know it was a frivolous act but one of their workers tried to sell us some bad work. Once I got wind of it, the head nigga agreed to reimburse me. When it was time to make the drop, we robbed them and took all three hundred bricks. At first, they didn't know it was me but they put a price on the streets for whoever had info. One of my own fucking workers dimed me out.

Brook had just got knocked by twelve, and at that point, I didn't trust nobody so I knew going to war with them niggas would be a mistake. Them niggas didn't want money, they wanted bloodshed and if it wasn't me, then it would have been you and the kids."

As I spoke, Lydia listened and observed closely. She only nodded her head as the tears ran down her face.

107

"I know you think I'm some kind of fucked up nigga, ma, but I couldn't afford to lose yall. Them niggas think I'm dead, but I know sooner or later, they'll find out I'm alive. This time, I'm ready for they ass, though. I'ma move you and the kids out of here and truthfully speaking, I'ma go to war with 'em."

The moment I said that she began to cry harder. I felt so bad, but shit, I made my bed so I had to lay in it. One thing I wasn't was a bitch and the only reason I really hid out was because this bitch ass nigga Que was the one behind my so called death. Stupid ass nigga thought he killed me, but that's the part I would leave out, for now.

I went to sit beside her because she was crying nonstop. It seemed like every tear that fell, the more I felt like shit, but Lydia had to understand I had my reasons.

"Stop crying, ma, please."

"I'm sorry about everything, Bronx. I mean you were gone for years. I was alone…" Before she could finish, I cut her off.

"Look, let's put that behind us," I said and she shook her head up and down. "Do you still love a nigga, Ly

108

Ly?" I said, calling her by her nickname I gave her when we first met.

"Yes! Yes, Bronx, I could never stop loving you," she began to cry again.

"So, what's up with you and ol boy?"

"Honestly, I haven't dealt with him since then. He just calls me, but I told him I couldn't mess with him because my husband would be here," she spoke, and then looked at me for verification.

"Do you want a nigga here?"

"Of course, I do."

"Well, guess what, ma. Daddy's home," I said and pulled her close to me.

***

After talking to Lydia, I felt relieved. It felt like a ton of bricks lifted off my shoulders. I led her up to the room and gave her what she had been missing for all these years. I fucked her ass into a straight coma, which is what she was doing now. I admired her while she slept. Her once short hair cut was now long and curly. It was sprawled out over her pillow and she still possessed the same beauty from when I first laid eyes on her. I ain't gone lie, I missed my wife like a muthafucka. True, I was in love with Cash and thought about her the entire time I was away, but after last night, seeing her with my brother, I knew I had to fall back.

The constant ringing of Lydia's phone knocked me out my daze. I shook her a couple times to tell her to answer it but she didn't budge so I retrieved it off the dresser and answered.

"Yeah?"

"Hello? Um, Lydia?" the male voice spoke into the phone.

"Nah, you got the wrong number," I spoke.

He huffed and puffed into the phone, and then hung up. After a few minutes, he called back and now Lydia was wide awake, staring at me with a shameful look.

110

"Man, answer your phone and tell your little boyfriend that daddy back home, so don't call no more."

She looked at me and then answered like she was unsure. I couldn't hear what he was saying but she told him exactly what he needed to know and hung him up.

"Lydia, call and change your number, yo. I'm not asking you, I'm telling you," I said then lifted off the bed and headed to the shower.

Chapter 9

Brooklyn Nino

These last couple of months couldn't have gotten any better. Cash and I would be planning the biggest wedding of the century and my next plan was to put a baby up in her. Watching how my brother interacted with his kids and wife only made me want kids more than I did before.

I was happy to see Bronx and Lydia patch their relationship up. It felt like everything was at peace in our lives. Ms. Lopez was back running her traps so that gave me and Cash more time to be with each other. However, since Que was locked up, Cash had to now fill in his shoes. I could tell Ms. Lopez wanted Cash out of the game, shit, I wanted her to fall back too. But, who were we kidding, Cash Muthafuckin' Lopez the biggest d-girl in the entire state.

112

"Hello?" I answered my ringing phone. I almost didn't answer because of the weird out of state number, but fuck it.

"Hello, Nino?" the woman spoke with a heavy accent.

"Yeah, who is this?"

"It's Gabriela."

"Gabriela?" I asked, puzzled.

"Yes, I was in the states with your brother, Bronx."

"Oh ok, yeah. What's up?"

"I have something I want you to see. You give me address, I send in mail," she spoke in her broken English.

I was iffy as to why would she want my address because this chick didn't even know me. However, I figured it had to be important so I shot her the address to one of my traps. After giving her the address, she hung up and I brushed the shit off, going on about my day.

After getting dressed, I headed to Nina's grand opening to meet Cash. When I arrived, she wasn't nowhere in sight so I went to holla at Carlos and mingle with everyone else. After a couple hours went by, I shot Cash a text because her ass still wasn't here and Nina asked about her a million times.

Me: Damn, ma, WYA? You about to miss the whole grand opening.

As soon as I closed my phone, she texted back.

My Wife: I'm sorry. I just left the cave, I'm on my way.

Me: Ok…

I couldn't help but laugh. My baby was indeed a real Trap Gyrl. She had been in the cave all day cooking up work with Ms. Lopez. Her ass left out the house at six this morning and here it was 4:00 in the evening and she was just now wrapping up. I understood how the game went, but after all the shit Cash had been through, I really wanted her to fall the back.

Cash

I was speeding on the freeway, trying to get to the grand opening. I knew Nina would kill me if I missed it, but I had to help my mother cook up the work to distribute for this week. Now that Que was in jail and Arcelie bitch ass was out the picture, it was just pretty much me, Mommy, and Dre left to cook. I cooked up as much work as I could and hurried out so I wouldn't be later than I already was. I took ten bricks with me so I could just cook the rest at home. I hated riding around dirty but this would be the chance I was taking to make the event. I

had my Mozzy "Bladadah" blaring through my car speakers, going at full speed. Looking in my rearview mirror, I noticed a patrol car behind me so I turned my music down a bit and tried to drive normal. The car trailed me for about two miles and then turned on the lights. Shit! This was just what I needed. I knew my rights, my license and registration were clean so I'd accept my ticket and gone about my business. Looking in my rearview mirror, I could see the cop approaching my vehicle. When he got to my driver side window, I cracked it and already had my driver license peeking through the crack.

"Ma'am, can you step out of the vehicle?"

"No, I can't, officer. Here's my license, just give me my ticket," I spoke, politely.

"Step out of the car, now!" he shouted, but I wasn't budging.

"I'm sorry, but I have somewhere to be. Please, just give me my…"

He cut me off and pulled out his firearm.

"Step out of the vehicle, now!" he shouted again.

Finally, I stepped out and put my hands on my hips. Now I was beyond annoyed, but I prayed he didn't open the trunk. He quickly threw the handcuffs on me and led me to the patrol car.

"Why am I being arrested?"

"You have a $30,000 warrant."

What the fuck! I thought to myself but remained quiet.

The officer pulled off with me in the backseat without another word. I wasn't tripping because I knew Brook would come bail me right out, and I was just glad he didn't open my trunk.

After about two hours of driving, I asked the officer over and over, where the fuck were we headed and the cracker muthafucka didn't bother to respond, once. My phone was in my jacket pocket so I couldn't reach it to call Brook but the moment we stopped, I would quickly call him. We pulled up into a neighborhood in the suburbs but on the other side of where me and Brook lived. We then pulled up to a huge white house and now I was really puzzled. He snatched me out of the car, forcefully and led me into the home.

When we made inside, he led me into the first bedroom and made me have a seat on the steel chair. I didn't know what the fuck was going on but this shit was getting beyond crazy. He then began to search my pockets and retrieved my phone. I watched him as he slid it into his top pocket and then left the room without a word.

Damn, not again. I thought to myself at just the thought of being kidnapped again only this time, I was sure I wouldn't make it out alive.

117

"Cash muthafucking Lopez," a male voice entered the room with a huge smile spread across his face.

I shook my head repeatedly. I don't believe this shit.

The moment he got closer to me, I coughed up the biggest loogie and spit in right in his face. This shit was like déjà vu, only this time I stared into the face of Mike.

"Hello, snitch boy," I said and smirked. I knew I was gambling with my life because Mike was trained by my team and we made sure we trained soldiers.

"Snitch boy, huh," he laughed. "Well, watch how much I snitch when we get rid of you, hoe. Oh, yall thought yall was coming for me, huh? Oh, bitch ass Blaze and your little boyfriend ain't here to save yo ass…"

"What the fuck you want, Mike? I can pay you more than these pigs paying you because I'm sure you're on their payroll."

"It ain't even about the money, it's about my freedom. I'm going to kill you now, then Brooklyn, and then I'll be able to get Que's bitch ass life in jail. I'll be five-mill richer and living in another country. Oh, let me

118

not forget Blaze's hoe ass while he's laid up with my thot ass wife, thinking he's doing something."

"He must be doing something you couldn't do because Tiny in love with a real nigga now. You ain't shit, Mike, but a snitch and bitch nigga, and my homegirl don't want no snitch!" I barked, but all he did was laugh. At this point, I didn't give a fuck, this nigga was a straight bitch and I'd die expressing how much of a hoe ass nigga he was.

Que

I walked down the hallway to retrieve my property. I was five minutes away from being a free man and this shit felt too good to be true. Just like Diane's friend promised, I was now on my way to society. It was crazy how the game worked. One million dollars and these muthafuckas would put their jobs at risk. Judge Jones got a nigga out, even before my court date. I don't know how she did it but I wouldn't question it, I was just happy to be out that bitch. I had shit to do starting with my dope head baby mama, and then I had to figure out what I would do about Deputy Williams. For now, I just wanted to smoke a fat blunt and max out.

When I got outside to the car, I was so disgusted with this bitch Keisha, I didn't even bother to say two words to the hoe. I wanted to reach over and smack the shit out the bitch but I held my composure, at least until we got home.

"Where my phone at, Keish?" I asked her, nonchalantly.

She went into her purse and pulled it out, but smirking as she handed it to me.

"Yo?" Blaze answered on the third ring.

"Nigga, I'm out that bitch!"

"Yoooo, you out, nigga?"

"Yeah, nigga! I'm calling you, ain't I?"

"Ha ha, fuck you, nigga," Blazed joked. "That's what's up. Aye, man, it's some crazy shit going on right now. Cash has been MIA for damn near 24 hours, we starting to get worried about her."

"Yo, tell me you are fucking joking?"

"Shit, I wish I was, man."

"Man, you sure she ain't ducked off with that nigga Carter somewhere?" I joked, but I was dead ass serious. Ricky was dead now so who else was there that could be bold enough to go after Cash.

"Nah…shit, Carter been with his bro all day."

"Damn, man. I'ma call you right back," I told Blaze and quickly hung him up.

I went into my phone's tracker and began entering my passcodes. I just prayed this dumb bitch Keisha hadn't deleted it. Bingo! I was logged in and got an address across town. I knew if Cash was being a little thot, she would be mad, but shit, I had to take my chances.

"Keisha, pull over, I need to drive this muthafucka," I told her and she did just that.

I went straight home and grabbed my strapped, then hopped right back on the freeway and headed towards Brickell Ave.

121

When we pulled up to the address that was on the tracker, I dead the engine and sat patiently waiting for some sort of movement in the home.

I know this ain't this bitch ass nigga? I asked myself, looking at Mike.

Cash was beside him, sitting in a chair. It appeared her hands were tied because I didn't see any hand gestures from her. I pulled out my piece and tried to get a clear shot. Focusing on my target, I then noticed another figure who appeared to be a white man standing in the doorway. Damn! I knew if I bodied Mike, he would probably shoot Cash, so I had to wait until my chance. After about 10 minutes later, the man left the room and this was my chance.

"Keisha, jump in the driver seat and leave the car running, alright?" I spoke and she just nodded her head yes. When she was secured in the driver seat, I went for the gusto…

Cash

"If you're going to kill me, why the fuck you ain't did it yet?" I barked at Mike. I was tired of sitting here staring at this muthafucka. This nigga up to something, I thought to myself because if he really wanted me dead, I would have been hours ago.

"Just shut the fuck up, bitch! Trust me, I'm ready to body your ass and get this shit over with too," he shouted.

A few seconds later, a smirk crept across my face because an infrared beam was pointed on the side of this niggas head. Any minute now he would be a dead man. I knew sooner or later Brook would come for me, I just wondered what the fuck took him so long.

"What the fuck you smiling at, hoe?" Mike asked, suspiciously, right when Splack! That nigga's head burst open like a watermelon and his body hit the ground.

The cop must have heard the impact of the window shutter and Mike's body hit the ground because he burst into the room.

"What the fuck!" he asked, then ran back out the room.

Seconds later, I heard the front door cave in, followed by two more shots.

"Que!" I asked as if I was dreaming.

He stood there with a sly grin, and then ran over to me and began un-cuffing me.

"Come on, wifey, before the pigs come," he shouted and I jumped straight to my feet.

On my way out the door, the cop laid lifeless. I bent down to grab my phone out his pocket and then followed Que out the door.

When we got outside, Keisha was parked out front with a puzzled look.

"Go, go, go, Keish!" Que said in a hurried tone.

Keisha made a complete U-Turn and headed towards the highway.

The entire drive, this bitch kept looking at me devilishly in the rearview mirror. What's this hoe problem? I asked myself but left it alone.

124

I then looked over at Que and he had a worried look on his face. I couldn't help but smile because Diane's friend came through for us. I was happy as hell to see Que. However, I did wonder how the fuck he found me, but I left it alone, for now.

When we pulled up to me and Brooklyn's home, I noticed Blaze, Nina, and even Marcus' car parked out front. They must be looking for me, I smiled to myself, knowing that was the reason Marcus was there.

When I opened the door, Nina was the first to spot me. She had a look on her face that read, Bitch!

"You know you gon be the death of me, Cash Carter," Nina said, smiling widely.

"I'm sorry," I whined, playfully.

"Que!" Nina shouted and ran towards Que for a hug. She then began calling for Brook and Blaze, and they ran into the living room full speed.

I stood back with a smirk while looking at Brooklyn. He just shook his head and then walked over to give Que a pound.

125

"Que, how the fuck you? Man, you wild, boy, you wild," Blaze said to Que like he knew something I didn't know. Blaze then looked at me while shaking his head. "Aye Nino, Cash on restriction. Don't let her out your sight, yo, she gone give a nigga a straight fucking heart attack," Blaze said and then walked out the house.

After we explained everything to Brook from beginning to end, he was relieved to know Mike was now dead. Therefore, Que would be walking from his case and again, we could go on with our lives. Que left, saying he had to throw out the trash at home. I didn't know what it meant, but what I did know was he was out and I was beyond happy to be back home.

Chapter 9

Cash

It had been two weeks since my abduction by Mike. Brooklyn wouldn't let me out his sight, and I wasn't even tripping because with all the shit I've been through this last year, I didn't want to leave his side.

I watched Brooklyn as he came out his clothes. He had a bottle of Ace in his hand and was climbing in the hot tub to join me. He lit his Cuban Cigar and laid back sitting across from me. When he looked up at me, his sexy smile sent goosebumps down my spine. He then hit his cigar. I watched him closely as he took a swig from the bottle. His dreads were pinned up to the top of his head and the beads from the steaming water slid down his chest, and that shit made my pussy throb.

"What, ma, why you eye fucking a nigga like that?" he smiled.

127

"What, I can't look at my fiancé?" I smirked shyly.

"Come here then, and show big daddy some love," he said and I did just that.

I stood up to give him a peep show and slid beside him. He pulled me close to him and instantly slid his hands between my legs. He started fingering my clit with his index finger, causing me to moan instantly. He slid me up in one swift move and sat me on the railing of the jacuzzi tub. He buried his face between my legs. I tilted my head back and prepared myself for the orgasm I was about to receive. He was making his tongue go in a circular motion. My legs were shaking and my body was having hot flashes. I wrapped my hands in his dreads and pushed his head deeper into my opening. After about 10 minutes of my body going through convulsions, I was ready for his magic stick. I pushed his head back and stood to my feet. I bent over without a word and he knew exactly what to do.

Brooklyn and I fucked for what seemed like forever until my pussy was throbbing. We were sweating profoundly, so we got out and headed to our bedroom. We climbed in bed, fully naked, and I cuddled right up under him.

"When you gonna start planning the wedding?" he asked while stroking my hair.

"Are you ready for me to start, Brook?"

"Hell yeah, ma. Shit, if it was up to me, we'd be going to the city hall and just get married. I'm not worried bout no big ass wedding but I know that's the shit yall women love."

"Yes, and you're helping too, punk."

"Anything for my Lil Mama," he said and began kissing me like we were starring in a romantic movie.

***

The next morning, Brooklyn left to go check some traps so I laid in bed, bored. I flipped through the TV, in search of something to watch. I began to get annoyed because we had cable, a Fire Stick, and Netflix, but I couldn't seem to find anything entertaining. It was a Sunday so I had another day to watch Love & Hip Hop so for now, I would just go on my Facebook and scroll my timeline.

I had promised Brook I wouldn't leave the house without him but I was so tempted to at least go see my mother. After about six rings, her phone went to voicemail so I tried again and the same thing. I then dialed Pedro and he let me know she had gone to Esco's house. I was so bored, I grabbed my keys and headed to Esco's mansion. Brooklyn had informed me that they didn't tell my mother I was missing because they didn't want to worry her, and I thanked God because she would have nearly had a heart attack.

When I pulled up to Esco's house, I was let right into the gate by his security. I walked into the home and wandered down the long hallway to his business room where I assumed they were. I knew Esco was her boy, but it was weird she was here and we were loaded with work. When I got to the door, it was ajar. My mother was screaming at the top of her lungs. I stood there and listened in at the two go back and forth.

"It's time to tell her, she deserves to know!" Esco shouted.

"Don't tell me what my daughter needs, Esco. She's been fine all these years."

"She's my daughter too! So, it's not just about you, Lopez," Esco shouted, calling her by her last name.

Daughter? What the fuck is going on?

I stood there stunned at what Esco just said. I wanted to believe that my ears were deceiving me but I knew exactly what I had heard. I stormed into the room and they both jumped at my presence.

"Hey, Mija?" my mother said, running to me for a hug.

I stepped back to decline. She gave me a worried look and when I looked at Esco, he had his head down.

"So, is it true, mom?" I shouted, looking from her to Esco, and back to her.

The moment she looked at me, her eyes told it all. My eyes began to water and I couldn't stand there any longer. I ran out of the room as fast as I could, straight to my car. The tears flooded my face. My hands were shaking so bad, I dropped my keys. I quickly gathered myself,

131

grabbed my keys, and hopped in my car. I needed to get far the fuck away from them before I lost it.

This shit is crazy! I said to myself as I pulled out of the gates of Esco's home.

Que

Keisha was standing in the living room, shouting and shit as if I would have a change of heart. It had been two weeks since I been home. The minute I got home after the whole incident with Cash and Mike, I had kicked the bitch Keisha out my house. She was ducked off at her mother's crib, that I bought, and that's exactly where the bitch would stay. Of course, she denied being on that shit but I was no dummy. Every time I saw her when I picked up my daughter, the bitch's eyes were glossy like she was out of it. Most of the time, I would be picking my baby from Keisha's mom and her mom would always say she hasn't been there all night. The bitch was doing dope head shit like begging for money but I refused to give it to her because I knew exactly what she would do with it.

"Nigga, I'm taking my baby home!" She was screaming and annoying my fucking soul.

"For what, to leave her with your mom! Nah, my baby staying right here with me!"

133

"Nigga, you gone give me my fucking baby!" she said, trying run upstairs to Qui's room.

"Bitch, you must have sniff too many lines. My daughter not going with your hoes ass, now get the fuck out my crib!" I jumped up in her face and she began to cry harder.

This bitch thinks I'm playing, I thought, jumping up in her face right when I heard pounding at my front door.

"Get your shit and roll up outta here, Keish," I told her, walking off towards the front door.

When I reached the door, I was stopped dead in my tracks. I looked back to see where Keisha was. When I noticed she wasn't there, I opened the door while shaking my head.

"So this what it is, Quintin?" Deputy Williams asked with aggression.

Fuck! this just what I needed, I sighed.

I looked down her stomach to see was she showing and indeed, her little belly poked out. I just prayed Keisha wouldn't notice it if her nosy ass came to see who it was at the door.

"How the fuck you know where my crib at?" I asked, forgetting this bitch had my entire name, address, birthdate, and probably my social security number.

"So you just say fuck me?"

"Man, it ain't like that, I just been busy, ma," I said, right when Keisha nosey ass walked up mugging me and Ms. Williams.

"Who's this bitch?" Keisha shouted for the ten-thousandth time today like she was my bitch.

Ms. Williams watched me closely but didn't say one word.

"Who is she, Que?"

"Man, just gone, Keisha."

"Just gone? Just gone? I'm not going anywhere until you tell me who's this bitch!"

"I ain't gotta tell you shit! You not my bitch!"

"Um, who are you?" Keisha looked at Ms. Williams, ignoring everything I just said.

"Ask him," Ms. Williams nodded her head in my direction.

I ain't gone lie, I see why Keisha was intimidated. Ms. Williams was looking sexy as a muthafucka. This was my first time seeing her in plain clothes and she had my dick hard as a bitch. I eye fucked her since she had been standing here, and now I wanted to hit that sweet pussy but Keisha was blocking a nigga.

"Go in the back," I demanded to Ms. Williams.

She smiled before walking off and Keisha really flipped out. I drug her ass out my house and forcefully shoved her ass in the car. She kicked, screamed, and called me every name in the book but that didn't stop me from getting her the fuck away from me.

By the time I made it into my home, I headed to the back to find Ms. Williams. She was sitting on my bed, waiting patiently. I couldn't help but laugh at the look she wore. These hoes are crazy. I laughed to myself.

"Man, take that shit off," I said, not wasting any time.

At first, she looked like she wanted to protest, then thought about it and started taking off her clothing. I came up out my pants in a hurry. I wasn't wearing a shirt so next was my Polo boxer briefs and I'd be knee deep in her pussy. Ms. Williams watched me closely with lust in her eyes. I could tell she wanted every last inch deep up in her.

Seconds later, I was plunging in and out her warm pussy. She was on the bottom and throwing it back like she was trying to prove a point. I matched her rhythm but pounding harder because I wasn't the type of nigga to let a chick out fuck me. She was staring me dead in the eyes and her eyes said so much. Next thing I knew, she started crying and shit. At first, I was gonna keep going but this shit was a major turn off. Therefore, I stopped stroking and gave her a look that said, What the fuck!

"What's up with the tears and shit, ma?"

"What you mean, Quintin? You know what's up. You've been out a couple weeks and you haven't bothered to even reach out to me," she cried.

I just rolled off her because I saw where this shit was going. I didn't know what she was thinking but she was just something to do in jail. These hoes were working with

137

feelings and that shit wasn't cool. The only woman that held my heart was Cash and they knew that shit, everybody knew this shit.

"You not thinking about keeping that baby, are you? I asked, skipping straight to the point.

She looked at me with the saddest eyes and that was confirmation she was indeed trying to keep it.

"Yes! I want my baby!"

"I'm not in any position to have any more kids. My fucking daughter in her room sleep right now, do you see what I just had to deal with her mother?"

"So, basically, fuck how I feel about the situation."

"I'm not saying that, but why would you keep it?"

"Nigga, you knew what could happen fucking me raw!"

"And, you knew what could happen so why you wasn't taking any birth control?" I asked, shaking my head. This bitch was now pissing me off. I lifted up and began putting on my clothes.

"So that's just it, huh, Quintin?"

138

"Man look, just do what you gotta do," I said, reaching in my dresser drawer. I pulled out a stack of money and threw it to her. By the look on her face, she knew exactly what is was for; a fucking abortion.

I then heard footsteps in the front of my house. Qui wasn't walking, so I knew it wasn't her. I grabbed my strap and told Ms. Williams to hush. I made my way down the hall and bumped into Cash, she was crying hysterically.

Damn she used her key, I thought to myself.

Cash was the only woman that had keys to my crib, not even Keisha had keys. That bitch was using my house keys that I left her when I had first got knocked and the minute I got out, I confiscated them with the quickness.

"What the fuck, Wifey?" I said, tucking my strap into the waistline of my jeans.

"Que, oh my God," she cried.

"Man, what's up? You scaring me, ma."

She then dropped her head and I could see her tears falling onto her lap. I almost forgot Ms. Williams was here until she walked in, fully clothed. She looked from me to Cash and just shook her head. She stormed out the house and I didn't even bother to chase her. The love of my life sat in front of me with tears in her eyes and this was the only thing that mattered right now.

"I'm sorry, Que," she said, referring to Ms. Williams.

"Nah, you straight, ma. Now, holla at me."

She began to explain to me what happened at Esco's house. She heard her mother and Esco mention she was Esco's daughter. All I could do was drop my head.

"Oh my God, you knew?" she asked, looking at me stunned. Looking her in her eyes, I guess I gave myself up.

She stood up and began backing away from me.

"Cash," I called out for her, but she shook her head repeatedly and stormed out.

At that moment, I felt like shit. I knew Cash belong to Esco a long time ago. I promised Ms. Lopez I wouldn't say a word and I kept my promise all these years. It had been plenty times I wanted to just tell Cash, but that wasn't my place. I worked for Ms. Lopez when Cash was young so I owed Ms. Lopez just as much loyalty as Cash.

This just not my day, I thought to myself, lifting off the couch.

I went into my daughter's room to check on her and then went back to my room. I rolled me a fat blunt and laid on my bed in deep thought for the remainder of the night.

Life! Was my last thought before I drifted off to sleep.

Chapter 10

Cash

By the time I made it home, my vision was blurred and I couldn't stop crying. The pain was unbarring. I was upset with my mother, Esco, and even Que.

Esco, my father? I cried as I searched the house for Brook.

Now it all made sense to me the more I thought about it. My father had died when I was younger. As I got older, anytime the subject about my dad came up my mother would act nonchalant. I always took it as she didn't want to talk about it because she was still hurt but truth be told, she was suffering from her infidelity.

I climbed into my bed and balled up in a fetal position. I couldn't stop crying because I had been lied to and felt deceived. Brooklyn came out of the restroom and rushed to my side. I was so out of it. I barely heard him speak.

"What's wrong, why?" he asked in a worried tone.

I just looked at him and shook my head. Right when I was gonna tell him what had happened, my mother started calling my phone. After ignoring her call twice, Esco began to call and I ignored him as well.

"Brooklyn, oh my God," I cried.

"What, ma? What happened?"

"Esco… Esco… oh my, gosh!

"Cash, talk to me, ma. You got a nigga worried."

"Esco is my father!" I shouted, not being able to hold it in any longer.

"What the fuck you mean Esco your father?"

"Exactly what I said," I replied then began to tell him the entire conversation I had heard between Esco and my Mother.

143

By the time I was finished, Brooklyn sat motionlessly. All he kept saying was, "This shit is crazy," which was exactly my thoughts.

Boom! Boom! Boom! Boom!

There was knocking at the door. I knew more than likely it was my mother. Honestly, I wasn't in the mood to be bothered, I needed time to myself and time to grasp the entire situation at hand.

Brooklyn went to open the door because it seemed as if she wouldn't give up and just leave. I slowly walked down the hallway to face what was ahead of me. As bad as this shit hurt, I needed answers.

When I walked into the living area, my mother stood side by side with Esco. I just looked at the two with an evil eye, waiting for one or the other to start talking. I guess because this was my mother's demise, she spoke up quick, fast, and a hurry.

"Cash, I'm so sorry you had to find out the way you did," she said and looked at me with pleading eyes. "I wanted to sit you down and explain everything to you from beginning to end, but it's too late. When me and Pablo were together, he cheated on me but being a fool, I stayed. After

144

he began to get sloppy with his affair, I finally stepped out on him."

"With Esco?" I said in a sassy tone, already knowing the answer.

"Yes, with Esco. Look, Mija, I was a boss bitch, the same boss bitch you are today. The same way you not going for a man disobeying you, I wasn't having that shit either. You could be upset for me not telling you, but judging me is what you won't do because you are a split image of me. After Pablo found out I had cheated, he figured you weren't his child. He loved you so much and did so much for you, he made me promise to never tell you," she then looked from me to Esco and then finished. "For a long time, I never told Esco you were his child. Esco to had a wife and I wasn't the type to break up a happy home because mine was broken. I finally told Esco you were his child when I first went to jail because I needed him to protect you in these streets."

That's why he wanted me out the game, I thought to myself as it all began to make sense.

The moment she said it, I noticed Esco drop his head. I felt relieved, but that still was pretty fucked up they would keep this all a secret from me.

"Who all knew?" I asked between tears.

My mother looked at me and spoke sheepishly.

"Que, Pedro, and Esco's security team at his home," she said, and it really started registering.

That's why they would always let me right through the gate. And this is exactly the reason Esco paid off the police to leave me alone. All along this nigga was my fucking father.

"Bae, you straight?" Brooklyn asked, knocking my thoughts back.

"Yes, I'm fine, bae."

"Cash, please forgive me, Mija," my mother asked with pleading eyes.

I just looked at her and nodded my head but I was so drained, I just agreed to whatever it was she was saying.

Brooklyn Nino

I was in traffic on my way to Trap Gyrl to take Cash some lunch. Afterward, I had to head to my trap house to holla at Kellz and collect the dough for the week. Over the last few days, shit had been crazy with the whole Esco being Cash's dad.

That's why that nigga wouldn't give me her number that day. I laughed to myself.

This shit was beyond crazy. All along, Cash's dad was a fucking billionaire and holding out with all the work. Cash was distraught at the whole situation but she was pretty much over it.

Driving on the highway bumping my Future "Rich Sex" I thought about Cash and our wedding. She wanted a big ass wedding, that I wasn't all up for but to make my baby happy I would do anything. Just the decorations alone ran me a quarter of a million but I was marrying a true fucking princess so any penny spent would be worth it. As I pulled up to the shop It was damn near nowhere to park so I pulled in Cash's other parking spot that was reserved in the front. I hopped out and made my way in to find my baby, but couldn't help but laugh at Monique doing a client's hair with a black eye.

"What you laughing at, bae?" Cashed asked, taking the food from my hands.

"Mo's thot ass, honestly," I said, and Cash began to laugh, already knowing why.

"Yeah, some little bitch name Raine that Ryder fucks with, tapped that ass," she laughed. I knew it had to be something that had to do with a nigga because that was her forte.

"That bitch still ain't learned."

"Once a thot, always a thot."

We both laughed together.

"Aye, look ma, I gotta head to the spot to collect. Go home when you done, so I could take you out tonight, alright?"

"Ok, where we going?"

"Don't worry bout all that," I said and kissed her on the head.

I walked out the shop and hopped straight on the highway. When I made it to the trap, I noticed a few cars there I'd never seen. I bounced out and made my way in, knowing Kellz probably had company.

When I walked in, it was two chicks sitting on the sofa and Kellz was at the table rolling a blunt. The two chicks looked over at me with beaming eyes like a kid at Christmas, but I kept it pushing towards where Kellz was sitting.

"Nino! What's da deal, my nigga?" he said, giving me a pound.

"Same shit, man," I shook my head.

"Be right back, let me go grab the bags."

"Aight," I said and walked to the fridge for a bottled water.

When I lifted up out the fridge, the girls were standing there smiling. The darker one must have been Kellz's piece because she only chuckled. The lighter chick tried her hand and began her bullshit macking.

149

"Damn, why Kellz never told me about you?" she asked, flirtatiously. No lie, she was pretty as a muthafucka. If I wasn't engaged, I'd probably knock her socks back.

"Because, I ain't nobody, ma, that's why. Now watch out."

"Damn, he rude," the darker girl said.

"He must got a bitch," the lighter girl barked, causing the other girl to laugh.

"First off, I ain't got no bitch, I got a wife so let's get that clear! Second, you or this bitch put together couldn't amount to her so I suggest y'all fallback."

The moment I finished my statement, they looked at me in shock. See, I'm not a rude type of nigga, but these hoes didn't know me and the way they approached me screamed THOT.

"You don't know what I got?" the darker girl said, offended.

"What you got, ma?" I asked, curious. "That raggedy ass Honda Accord outside?" I shot at her and laughed right in her face.

150

Kellz walked back in on the end of the statement and began laughing. They both looked stunned but didn't say shit else. Kellz handed me three duffle bags full of dough and a yellow envelope.

"This came in the mail for you too, my nigga," he said as I took the envelope from his hand with a curious look.

Oh, the package from Carter's bimbo, I thought to myself and slid it into one of the duffle bags. I then walked out but made sure I smirked at the two bitches before I left, causing Kellz to laugh again.

When I made it home, I went straight to my room and began to count my money. An hour and 19 minutes later, I was sixty-two thousand dollars richer. I quickly secured it into my safe and then headed downstairs.

Before I walked out, I grabbed the yellow envelope, curious to what it could be. I went into my theater room and poured me a drink. I knocked it back and then poured another one before I opened the envelope. When I finally cracked it open, it was a DVD that read, "Fuck you, Carter," on the front.

Oh, this bitch must be mad, I laughed to myself.

151

I popped it into the DVD player. Once the screen came on, I focused on what was on it. Cash was coming down a hallway on crutches. She then made it into what appeared to be a living room. My brother was sitting on a couch smoking a blunt and Cash took a seat right beside him. They talked for a minute and the way they looked at each other was making my blood boil. After a few minutes of talking, Bronx leaned in for a kiss and Cash accepted. By this time, I was standing to my feet. To say I was mad was an understatement, I was furious.

I paced the floor, ready to body both their asses. The way they looked at each other and the way they kissed, you couldn't tell me they hadn't fucked. I pulled out my phone and dialed Cash's number. I tried to hold my composure as I spoke.

"Cash, get home now!"

"I'm working, Brook, what's wrong?"

"I'm not gonna say it again!" I shouted into the phone and hung up.

I shook my head profoundly, I couldn't believe this shit. I poured me another shot and then sat back and waited for Cash's arrival.

152

Thirty-five minutes later, I could hear her heels clicking on the tile floor as she made her way throughout the house. I let her ass walk all around until she found me sitting with red eyes and a look of grimish. She ran over to me and sat down beside me. I didn't want to even be near her right now so I stood up and again and began pacing.

"Brook, what's wrong?" she asked with a scared look. Just the look alone made my heart sink but not today, she wasn't getting away with this one. In all honesty, I wanted to slap the shit out of her but putting my hands on a woman wasn't me.

"I'ma ask you one muthafucking time, Cash! Did you fuck my brother?" I barked.

She looked at me confused and shook her head no. "No, Brook, I told you I haven't fucked him. Why the fuck…"

I cut her ass off.

"It sure looks like it to me," I said and pressed play on the DVD.

Her eyes widened and she looked scared but already prepared for what she was about to see. The moment Cash

153

and Bronx kissed, she dropped her head and that was all the confirmation I needed. I looked at her with tears in my eyes. A nigga was heartbroken. I hadn't cried like this since her fake ass death and now, I was starting to think all the shit about her being kidnap was premeditated.

"Get the fuck out my house, yo!"

"Brook, I swear…"

"Just get the fuck out my shit, Cash!" I shouted, cutting her off.

She began to cry hysterically but that shit wasn't working today. She gave me one last look and then stormed off. It wasn't a surprise because Cash had so much pride I knew it would only take a few get out's and she would go.

The minute I knew she was far from my house, I shot her a text.

Me: The wedding is off! That was all I said and she didn't bother to even respond. I wanted to call Bronx so bad but I chose not to. I had so much pride just like Cash, I didn't want to look like a hater. To keep it one hunnit, Cash was his first, so how could he really be wrong.?

Fuck! I shouted, slamming the bottle of Hennessy into my eighty-inch television.

They could have just told me! I thought to myself and stormed upstairs to my bedroom.

When I got to my room, I kicked my shoes off and jumped in the bed. I grabbed my phone and did what Cash would usually do; post a status on Facebook.

What's on your mind?

Status: Bitches really ain't shit! 100...

I wanted her to see it. Hell, I prayed she would see it so she could understand exactly how I felt. At this point, I was glad I found out now, rather than after the fake ass marriage. That was another thing eating me up. I would have walked down that aisle with her scandalous ass and being the laughing stock of century.

Fuck that bitch, Bronx could have her. Hell, Que could have her, I'm through.

155

Chapter 11

Cash

It has been almost two months since the fall out with Brooklyn, and I was beyond stressed the fuck out. I texted him, called him, and even popped up at his traps. The few times I went to his house, he didn't bother to answer. However, I knew he was watching me on his home surveillance cameras.

I really didn't sleep with Carter…

I texted him, repeatedly. No matter how many times I texted, or what I said, he ignored me every time. Between the situation with my mom and Esco, and then this bullshit with Brooklyn, I was stressed the fuck out. Not to mention, I was just abducted twice and by someone I trusted with my life. I was tired of crying, so I kept my head up high and sucked it up like a boss.

Right now, I stood in the Cave's Kitchen, whipping twelve bricks and watched my mother who was now down to her last six. She watched me closely as she stirred the contents in her pot.

"Cash, you gotta go get your husband back," she spoke, looking from her Pyrex jar.

"He's not answering and I'm not about to keep tryna kiss his ass."

"It's not about kissing his ass, Mija, it's about not turning your back on someone you love when you're in the wrong. Don't get me wrong, I understand where you're coming from but imagine how Nino feels. Now, I believe you didn't sleep with Carter, but I mean the proof is in the pudding. As long as you don't plead your case, you look guilty. Take it from a woman who knows," my mother spoke, making me do something I promised I wouldn't do anymore, and that was to cry.

I knew everything my mother was saying was real, but I had pretty much given up on Brook. The way he ignored me and shut me out hurt me to the core. When he was getting his rocks sucked off by Tiffany while I was laid up with bullets wombs, I forgave him. He swore he didn't

157

fuck her and I believed him, but here he was pointing the finger.

As I stirred the product, my head began to spin and I suddenly felt nauseous. I ran, quickly, to the bathroom to give up my entire stomach. My mother ran to my aid and asked if I needed anything.

"Cash, are you with child?" my mother asked with her eyebrows raised.

I quickly shook my head no and kept calling Earl, collect. By the time I was done throwing up, my mother relieved me. I explained to her that it was the dope that was getting to me, but she gave me a sideways look like she didn't believe one word. I knew she was insinuating I was pregnant but I knew for a fact it was the dope.

***

When I made it to me and my mother's home, I went to my room and laid down, I was feeling horrible. Esco had some bomb as work and I assumed the fumes were getting to me. I went into my bathroom and turned on the shower. I was in much need of a shower message so I turned the nozzle on my shower head to massage my body. I couldn't do anything but sigh while getting into the hot shower, which was something I did every time I stepped in. I had gotten so accustomed to Brook, I didn't even shower alone anymore, so just like any other day, I missed him. Just the thought of him had me ready to tear up, but I quickly shook it off. I soaped up and hopped out, going to my dresser drawer for something to sleep in. I pulled out one of Brook's oversized t-shirts, slid it on, and climbed into bed.

The moment I became settled in, my phone began to ring. No lie I prayed it was Brooklyn but to my surprise, it was Carter. I simply ignored the call because I didn't have shit to say to him. He was the one who gave his brother that tape of us. I don't know what Carter was trying to prove, but he was beyond foul for that move.

I went to my Facebook and browsed through my timeline. I then went to Brook's page, sure he hadn't posted anything because he hated social media. When I clicked on his timeline and began reading his statuses, I got upset. The first status read, "Bitches really ain't shit." Then, there was another status that simply read "Lit," which let me know he was out in the world, somewhere drunk, and enjoying himself. I posted a status that read, "She ain't me," being petty because whatever bitch he was laid up with wasn't me and could never be me.

I curled up under my blanket and pushed the thoughts of Brooklyn out my mind. Tonight, I was going to sleep, Unbothered.

***

For the next couple days, I woke up feeling like shit. I ran to the bathroom repeatedly, throwing up my entire stomach, something I had been doing every morning. Because I couldn't blame it on the dope I wasn't cooking, I figured exactly what it was. My mother must have peeped game also because right now, she was standing in front of me with an EPT. She handed me the test without another word and then left as quick as she came. I braced myself for what the results would be.

It seemed as if that five minutes took forever. When I grabbed the test off the sink, I couldn't help but drop my head at the two lines it showed clear as day.

Fuck! I cursed myself.

I wasn't sure what I would do at this point, but I needed to call someone fast. I dialed Nina's number and like always, she picked up, quickly.

"Hey, boo?" she cooed into the phone.

"Hey, ma?" I said, half-hearted.

"Cash, don't be over there stressing, ma. Nino will come around soon."

"Ugh, it ain't even that, Nina."

"So, what's wrong?"

"I'm pregnant!" I barked, not being able to hold it in any longer.

"Oh my God!" she shouted like she was happy for me but as for me, I was stressed the fuck out about the whole situation. "Cash, I know you thinking bout killing that baby?" The tone of her voice changed.

161

"Honestly, I don't know what I'm going to do, Nina."

"Girl, Nino gone kill you!"

"I know, but shit, I'm not trying to raise this baby alone," I said, knowing damn well Nino would help. But fuck that, I didn't want to raise this baby not being his wife.

"Just give him some time. Don't do anything just yet."

"Nina, yo ass bet not tell him either."

"I'm not, I pinky swear."

After talking to Nina for a while, she filled me in on the date of her baby shower, which was a couple weeks away. I had been going through so much, I nearly forgot about her baby shower and not to mention, Brooklyn's birthday as well.

It took everything in my power to get out of my bed. I went downstairs to find some soup because anything else wouldn't stay on my stomach. I looked out the window and I could see my mother and Pedro sitting on the bench in front of our waterfall, talking. When my mother looked up, she spotted me and then smiled.

162

Knock. Knock. Knock.

Someone was at the door. I knew it had to be someone I knew because they had gotten past Pedro and the security gates. I quickly took my rubber band from my hair and shook it loose. I was trying my best to get halfway cute just in case it was Brook. When I got to the door, I couldn't help but roll my eyes. I opened the door, slowly, and Carter stared at me with an unknowing look.

"What, Carter?" I asked, walking back towards the kitchen.

Before I could make it, he snatched me by the arm and forced me to look at him.

"Cash, I didn't give that nigga the tape!"

"So, who gave it to him, Carter!"

"Man, it was that bitch Gabriela."

"Gabriela?" I asked, puzzled.

"The chick I had brought back with me. She watched everything on the tape from the first day I saved you, up until the day we came to the US. That bitch sent one to Lydia too," he shook his head.

163

"So, Lydia knows now?" I asked, feeling horrible.

"Yeah, I explained everything to her, but—"

Pow! Pow! Pow! Pow! Pow! Pow! Pow! Pow! Pow! Pow! Pow! Pow! Pow! Pow! Pow! Pow! Pow! Pow! Pow! Pow! Pow! Pow! Pow! Pow! Pow! Pow! Pow! Pow! Pow! Pow! Pow! Pow!

Carter snatched me to the ground right when the front windshield shattered. Oh my god! My mother, Pedro? I thought to myself and jumped to my feet.

"Cash, get down!" Carter yelled, pulling his gun from his waistband.

"My mother is outside, Carter!" I shouted and kept running for the front door.

There was a van at the entrance of the gate with a man standing near the passenger door, firing shots, and another man was standing at the back of the van, firing and ducking at the same time. The minute I reached my mother and Pedro, I hit the ground because they as well were busting back.

"Cash, stay down!" my mother shouted as she let off every last shot she had in her gun.

Boom! Boom! Boom! Boom! Boom! Boom! Boom! Boom! Boom! Boom! Boom! Boom! Boom! Boom! Boom! Boom! Boom! Boom! Boom! Boom! Pedro was running towards the gate firing shots into the van. Boom! Boom! Boom! Boom! Boom! Boom! Boom! Boom! Boom! Boom! Boom! Boom! Boom! Boom! Boom! Boom! Boom! Boom! Boom! Boom!

The guy that was behind the van fell to the ground so I assumed he was shot. The other shooter was struck in the shoulder so he quickly jumped back into the van and it sped off, leaving the body behind.

"Cash, are you ok?" my mother ran to me and began examining me from head to toe.

Carter stood with a worried look, but I simply shook my head to let them know I was fine. The fall caused me to sprain my ankle but after being shot twice a sprained ankle wasn't shit.

I limped my way into the house. My mother and Pedro followed me in. When I walked off, Carter was standing there with an upset look and it only meant shit was about to get ugly.

165

It was crazy how I was now with Brooklyn and it seemed as if Carter still had feelings for me. The look in his eyes when he snatched me down was a worried one and at that moment, I could tell he was still in love with me. My mother was on the phone, screaming at the top of her lungs. By the conversation she was having, I could tell if was my infamous dad, Esco.

After about 30 minutes, my mother walked back into the living room with a strange look. She looked from Carter to me, and then back to Carter. She simply shook her head and began speaking.

"Carter, I just spoke with Esco," my mother said with an eyebrow raised, still looking directly at Carter. "He spoke with some people and they said that the shooters were from the Carlito Cartel."

Carter just shook his head and I already knew exactly why.

Sitting with my mother and Carter, as he explained everything that had happened with the Cartel before he faked his death, my mother understood. She told him that she would handle it, and I knew exactly what that meant. I jumped to my feet because I could feel my stomach turning. I ran to the nearest restroom and began throwing up for the umpteenth time in the last week.

I couldn't help but cry because it hurt so bad. I hadn't eaten anything in two days so every time it came up, it was the lining of my stomach, which was being forced out my body. When I looked up, Carter was standing in the doorway with a look of hurt. I looked up at him, between red eyes, and I could tell he knew exactly what it was. He shook his head and then walked out. I just prayed he didn't tell Brooklyn.

When I made it back in the living area, to my surprise, Carter was still here speaking to my mother and Pedro. I went and took a seat quietly, making sure I didn't interrupt their conversation. I listened on as my mother gave Carter a few locations where the Carlito's hung out and even a few of their home addresses. I knew that information came from Esco, and I could only smile. Esco was the kind of man that didn't involve himself in any beef. He was too busy getting money so war was the last thing on his roster. I knew exactly why he was doing it and I couldn't help but smile.

Que walked into the front door, causing us all to look up. I don't know if I was tripping or not, but I swear it looked like Carter was reaching for his gun. They stared at each other with piercing eyes, I just prayed it wasn't about to go down between the two.

Chapter 12

Que

When Ms. Lopez called me, I knew something was wrong. She didn't want to speak over the phone so she told me to come right over. I jumped right up, slid into my clothing, and then grabbed my strap off my dresser, tucking it behind my waist. Not only did I need to see what was up with Ms. Lopez, but I needed to holla at Cash as well. I hadn't spoken to her since she found out I knew Esco was her father. I knew she was mad at a nigga, but today, I would make her understand my point of view.

When I walked into the home, I'd be damned. I thought to myself, looking Carter dead in his eyes. It looked like the nigga wanted to reach for his strap and I was pretty much ready. I had a hot twenty-one shots to put in his ass, and this time, I would be sure his ass was flat lined. The look Cash was giving me told me to fall back. But one hunnit, I was ready if he was.

169

This was my first encounter with the nigga since he'd been back from hiding. All the times he was around, I made sure to stay far the fuck away because I knew it would be beef on site. Now that Cash was with Nino and this was his brother, I knew shit could get real ugly so for the sake of Cash, I chose to just stay the fuck away.

Damn! I thought to myself, hoping it wasn't about me trying to kill Carter when he faked his death. To my surprise, it was actually about the Carlito's shooting up Ms. Lopez's house. I sighed in relief when she started explaining what happened and the entire time she spoke, Carter was watching me closely. Little did this nigga know I was about to have beef with them niggas too because now that he was still alive, they would come for my head because I didn't get the job done they had paid me to do.

"Que, are you listening?" Ms. Lopez asked, knocking me off my chain of thoughts.

"Yes, Ms. Lopez," I nodded my head.

She began rambling again but my mind was on something else. I was now puzzled as to why Carter was here and not Nino. I know this bitch ain't fucking this nigga now, I thought to myself while looking at Cash. I had heard that Cash and Nino were beefing and had broken up, but what I didn't know was why.

The ringing of my phone broke me out my thoughts. I looked down to see that it was Keisha so I sent the call to voicemail. She called again and this time, I was worried about my daughter so I excused myself from everybody and walked into the kitchen.

"Man, if my daughter straight, why the fuck you calling my phone?"

"So you about to have another baby, Que?" Keisha asked, annoying my fucking soul.

"Man, what the fuck you talkin bout, I ain't having no fucking baby?" I lied.

"Nigga, you know what the fuck I'm talking about!"

"Nah, I don't, really," I spoke nonchalantly.

"Your little bitch sent me an ultrasound picture. I swear, fuck you, nigga! You ain't never seeing my baby again. I'm packing right now and I swear the minute I'm done, we out this bitch!" she shouted into the phone, crying.

171

Before I could say anything, she hung up. This bitch was playing with my daughter and that's the one thing I hated. I'm about to go put my foot in this hoes ass, I thought, walking back into the living room.

Everybody had left, except Cash. She looked at me with pleading eyes so I took a seat beside her.

"Look, ma. I'm sorry for not telling you about Esco being your father."

"It's ok, Que. I have so much stuff going on in my life, I'm over the shit with Esco," she said, tucking her hair behind her ear.

"I'm glad you're ok, tho," I said, referring to the incident that took place earlier.

"Yeah, me too. That shit was crazy. All I could think about was my mom because she was outside. Once again, Carter was here to my rescue. The moment he snatched me down, a bullet came crashing through the window," Cash said and just the thought of Carter's name made my blood boil.

"You fucking with that nigga, Cash?" I just had to know.

172

She looked at me, then shook her head no. "No. And, you know I never lie to you, Que. But I haven't fucked with Carter like since before his death. Brooklyn left me because he saw a tape of us kissing when I recovered from the shooting. I swear, Que, that was all we did."

"So how the fuck Nino see the tape?"

"Carter's Brazilian boo," Cash smirked.

"Now I'm stuck, pregnant," she blurted out and began to cry.

I couldn't believe Cash was crying right here in front of me. This girl was a true soldier but I had to remember she still had feelings like everybody else. The mention of Cash saying she was pregnant blew me back, but how could I judge her, shit, I had a baby on the way and not to mention, by a fucking pig.

"So, what you gonna do, ma?"

"Honestly, I don't know," she said, between tears. "I think I'll just get rid of it."

I gave her a knowing look before I spoke. "Yeah, that might be the best thing," I said to her and pulled out my ringing phone.

You damn right I said it. Yall must have forgotten who the fuck I was. If she decided to keep it, I wouldn't be mad but fuck that, I had plans of us being together one day and with this nigga Nino out the picture now, I couldn't have her giving birth to his baby. I put one finger up to Cash to give me a minute. Like always, I put the phone on speaker so she could listen to this bullshit I was dealing with my damn self.

"Man, you foul as fuck, Stephanie!" I said, calling Ms. Williams by her first name.

"How I'm crazy, Quintin?"

"Why the fuck you send my BM the pic of your ultrasound?"

The minute I said it, Cash shot me a look.

"The bitch was playing on my phone."

"Man, you a fucking lie. Your thirsty ass got a hold of her number just like you got a hold of my address," I barked, shaking my head.

174

"Fuck you and fuck her, Quintin, that hoe could keep you!"

"Man, shut the fuck up because you know that's not how you feel. Go to the house and wait for me, I'll be there," before she could say another word, I hung up on her ass.

Cash then stood up to her feet, laughing. I guess she figured that was my cue to shake.

"I'ma see you later, ma."

"Ok…" She looked sad.

"Stop stressing, baby girl. You a soldier, remember?" I said, and pinched her on the tip of her nose, causing her to smile. I then walked out the door to go face the bullshit that waited with my punk ass baby mama.

Brooklyn Nino

"What's up, Blaze?" I said, answering my phone on the first ring.

"Yo, shit is wild."

"What happened now?"

"Nigga, the Carlito's shot up Ms. Lopez's house."

"Word? Is Cash straight?" I asked, and Blaze chuckled.

"Yeah, nigga, your wife straight. Nobody got hit."

"That's all I needed to know."

"Yeah, man, you know shit bout to get ugly out here."

"I'm already knowing," I said while shaking my head.

"Yo, who is that?" Blaze asked, puzzled because he heard Tiffany in the background, asking if I wanted her to make my plate.

"That ain't nobody," I replied nonchalantly, and again, Blaze chuckled.

"Nigga, Cash gone kill you."

We both laughed.

"Shid, I'm a free agent, my nigga. Cash should have thought about that when she was fucking my brother."

"Man, you know that girl ain't fuck him, Nino. If she said she didn't, you should believe her."

"Yeah, just like she had lied about Que?" I said, annoyed.

"Yeah, you got a point. But, what's up with your b-day?" Blaze asked, changing the subject.

"I'm having a cookout," I replied, thanking God Tiffany was in the kitchen. I for sure didn't want her there and I knew if she found out, she would most definitely pop her ass.

"Yeah, I feel you. Well, let me know and I'ma push thru there."

"Alright, I'll hit you with the addy the day of…"

"Aight, my nigga, stay up."

Aight, one."

Since I haven't been fucking with Cash, I pretty much been chilling and doing me. I started back fucking with my patnas heavy and of course, Tiffany got wind of me and Cash's break up so she wiggled her way back in. I knew I had no business fucking with her, but her head game was so sick and now that I was single, I could pretty much do what the fuck I wanted to. Not to put the hoe on no peddle stool because she wasn't half the woman Cash was, but Tiffany was mad cool and not to mention, she loved a nigga dirty draws. I actually found peace with her because she had a little cozy apartment that was ducked off, a nice little job, and she wasn't into the street life, other than fucking with D-Boys. A nigga wasn't trying to play house with Tiff or nothing, so she was pretty much just something to do, for now.

I'd be lying if I said I didn't miss Cash. I thought about her every day and night since the day she stormed out my house. My brother tried to ensure me that nothing happened with him and Cash, but it was hard for me to believe that, knowing how he felt about her.

Chapter 13

Blaze

"You ready, ma?" I asked Tiny, looking over at her in my passenger seat. When she cocked her strap back that was all the confirmation I needed.

I couldn't help but smile because this was a side of Tiny I'd never seen before. When she was with Mike, she used to do drops with him and even helped whip some work a few times but I've never known her to pop a strap. I couldn't help but smile because we were on some real Bonnie and Clyde shit and who else better to ride out with you than your down ass bitch. This shit with Tiny was making a nigga feel good inside. I felt like a whole new man and now, I understood why Cash and Nino were so in love. No lie, I was falling for this girl in a real way.

We pulled up to the building where the Carlito's held their meetings. Sitting in the car patiently waiting for these niggas, with our straps in hand, we sat quietly. I watched closely as one of the men in the entourage stepped outside to smoke a cigarette. I knew then that the meeting had to be over. Once Mario, the head of the cartel, stepped out the door followed by six more men, that was our cue.

"Scerrrrrrr!"

The sound of our screeching tires caused them to look our way, but it was too late.

Pop! Pop! Pop! Pop! Pop! Pop! Pop! Pop! Pop! Pop! Pop! Pop! Pop! Pop! Pop! Pop! Pop! Pop! Pop! Pop! Pop! Pop! Pop! Pop! Pop! Pop! Pop! Pop! Pop! Pop! Pop! Pop! Pop! Pop! Pop! Pop! Pop! Pop! Pop!

Pow! Pow! Pow! Pow! Pow! Pow! Pow! Pow! Pow! Pow! Pow! Pow! Pow! Pow! Pow! Pow! Pow! Pow! Pow! Pow! Pow! Pow! Pow! Pow! Pow! Pow! Pow! Pow! Pow! Pow! Pow! Pow! Pow! Pow! Pow! Pow! Pow! Pow!

I dropped two of them, instantly. One man ran Mario to their van and had him covered. I looked over at Tiny and she was still blazing, dropping who appeared to be the driver. Satisfied, we jumped back in the ride and pulled off, quickly. We both laughed as we did one hundred, getting away.

Them niggas didn't even get to shoot back.

After we ditched the rental car, we headed back to my crib. We hopped in the shower together and I couldn't even wait, I slid my dick straight up in baby girl, bareback and all. The way she was busting that strap had a nigga really in love and dick hard than a muthafucka.

After we stepped out, we laid in the bed completely naked. I rolled me a blunt and then I called Ms. Lopez. She quickly answered on the second ring. I wasn't worried about not getting Mario because we just wanted to send a message just like the one they had sent.

"Hey, Blaze."

"What's up, Ms. Lopez?"

"Oh, shit, here with Esco."

"Ms. Lopez, let me find out you and Esco all in love and shit."

We both laughed.

182

"He's in love, Blaze, you know I don't love these hoes," she said in her accent and again, we both laughed. We both knew that was a lie, though, because Ms. Lopez was open for Esco just like Esco was open for her.

"We put the kids to sleep. That's why I was calling."

"What about the nanny?"

"We relieved the nanny of her shift since all the other kids were sleep."

"Ok, good job, my boy."

Ok, Ms. Lopez. I'm about to tap this ass I got over here," I said, causing us to laugh again.

"Nasty ass, Blaze."

"Awe, Ms. Lopez, I know you ain't talking, Esco bout to bend that thang over."

"Hahaha," she laughed because she knew it was true. And just like that, she disconnected.

Tiny snuggled up in my arms the minute I hung up the phone. I flipped through the television, trying to find something to watch. I'd be damned, Stated Property was on, me and Cash's favorite movie. Once we fixed our self to get comfortable, I kissed the top of Tiny's head, ensuring her that I was indeed proud of her today.

"I love you, Blaze," she said, not even looking up at me.

I stroked her head a few times and then replied. "I love you too, Baby Girl," and I meant every word.

Nina

Standing in the mirror, twirling around, I had to admit, I was looking cute to be six months pregnant. I was rocking an Ashley Martin sun dress that showed my now hella big boobs. I couldn't wear heels so my feet were laced in some diamond sandals that strapped up my ankle. Nikki had my hair whipped up in a bob and with every move, it bounced. I had just opened up my boutique and it was doing really great, so I was beyond excited. With a little help from Instagram, Nina Cash was going worldwide and sales were growing rapidly.

I grabbed my Chanel bag and headed outside to hop in my baby blue Maserati. Once inside, I turned on my Rihanna CD and hopped on the highway to the Flat Line Projects. Carlos didn't know I was coming, but why would it matter, I was his one and only lady and not to mention, I would be giving birth to his baby soon.

Carlos and I hadn't found out the sex of the baby yet because Cash thought it was a good idea to save the news for the baby shower. I wanted a boy and to my surprise, Carlos wanted a baby girl. Honestly, it really didn't matter to Carlos because he already had two kids by his baby mama, Carissa. To my surprise, Carissa was pretty cool. We talked on the phone every time her kids were coming to spend time at the house. Even her husband was mad cool and he too would sometimes drop the kids off to Carlos.

When I pulled up to the projects, I went to Carlo's first trap house and he wasn't there. I then hopped back in my whip and drove towards their hang out, where most of the sales were made and all the D-Boys hung out. The minute I pulled up, I observed a dice game and a few bitches standing around, watching.

I zoomed in on Carlos, sitting on the stoop and my mouth hung to the floor. There was a little skin chick sitting between his legs. They both watched his phone and whatever he was scrolling at must've been interesting because they hadn't looked up once. My blood began to boil like a witch's pot. I stepped out my car, by passing the dice game and walked straight up to the two who looked mighty cozy.

When Carlos looked up he had a stunned look on his face and the bitch had the audacity to smirk. No lie, she was cute but she looked like around the way thot. Being pregnant, I was so emotional my tears began to fall, but I was a real trooper so I turned to walk away. Halfway to my car, Carlos grabbed my shoulder, causing me to spin around and face him. I gave him a look of grimace and was ready to pop off. Looking over him, the bitch had followed behind him and stood with her arms folded like she needed some kind of explanation.

"Get the fuck off me, nigga!"

"Man, Malina, it ain't even like that, ma."

"So, what the fuck is it like? Because clearly, I saw you and this bitch cuddled the fuck up," I shouted, pointing to the chick.

"That's the homegirl, ma," he said and the bitch smacked her lips.

I then shot her a look of death. "Bitch, why the fuck are you all in my grill?" I shouted at the hoe and the minute I said it, she ran past Carlos and tried to swing. I guess the hoe had me misconstrued because I was pregnant.

I stepped back and two pieced the bitch with face shots. Carlos snatched me back and before I knew it, he had slapped the bitch to the ground.

"Bitch, have you lost your mind!" he shouted at her.

She held her face with a look that said, she couldn't believe what he had just done. I laughed right in the hoe face and turned to walk away. By this time, the whole dice game had stopped and was in awe at what was going on.

"Fuck you, Carlos!" I spat, hopping in my car.

He ran up to my driver side, screaming for me to get out but I didn't have shit to say to him so I simply pulled off.

On the highway, I cried my eyes out. I wanted to go to Cash's house and tell her what happened but I was too embarrass so I simply headed home. When I got there, I went straight to my bed and cried until I couldn't cry anymore. I couldn't believe this nigga, but how could I doubt it. He was a typical nigga and I knew with living the street life it came with bitches. What hurt the most was that Carlos wanted this relationship, he asked for this baby and here he was about to throw it all away, for what?

Looking down at my phone, he was blowing it up constantly but I was done with his ass. I balled up under my cover, knowing he would come running but what could he really say? I changed the access code to my security gate because, without that, he couldn't enter. I was through with his ass, or at least that's how I felt at the moment.

Chapter 14

Cash

The Cookout...

I was in my room getting dressed. It was Brooklyn's birthday and through the grapevine, I heard his sister was throwing him a cook out. I knew I was taking a chance popping up but I wanted to talk to him about the baby and possibly see if we could work it out. I knew I had to get hella sexy, which wasn't hard so I browsed through my closet until I settled on the perfect outfit. I pulled out some stone washed holy shorts that were slightly shredded at the bottom. I settled on a short sleeve sweater shirt that hung off the shoulders by YSL. Because it was a cookout, I choose not to wear heels so I threw on my Balenciaga sneakers. My hair was flat ironed bone straight that I pushed to one side and let it hang long. I kept my jewelry simple and my make-up lightly laced. I put on my YSL shades and grabbed my YSL handbag to match and then headed for my ride. I chose to drive my G-Wagon because I loved how easy it was to get to Dolly. I pulled out my phone to call Nina and she answered, quickly.

"Hey, Boo."

"Hey, Cash."

"So are you coming with me, hoe?"

"Yeah, I'ma come with you. I'm actually ready, so how far are you?"

"I'm just leaving my house, so I guess you could head out and meet me there."

"Ok, I'm walking out now," Nina said and we hung up.

I turned on my Beyoncé Lemonade CD and jumped on the highway. For some strange reason, I had jitters and butterflies all at the same time. I hadn't seen Brook since our fall out and to my surprise, he hadn't even called to check on me after the Carlito's shot my home up. I prayed that Carter was at the cookout so he could ensure his brother that we hadn't slept together, I just prayed Brook would have believed him. I missed Brooklyn so much that

190

it hurt to think about it. I needed him next to me, and I hoped he would just hear me out so we could move forward. Getting off the freeway, Nina shot me a text saying that she was pulling up. I let her know I was five minutes away and would be there shortly.

Here we go, I sighed, preparing myself for whatever was about to happen.

When I pulled up, I spotted Nina's car. I found a parking spot right on the side of her.

This muthafucka is popping, I said to myself exiting the car.

It was all kinds of cars parked out front from foreign whips to low riders, but of course, because it was the infamous Nino's birthday.

"Bitch, it's popping," Nina said, walking up on me. Her stomach had grown so much since the last time I had seen her. She was looking cute herself and I loved the bob she was rocking.

We made our way into the yard but we were stopped three times by guys who were checking us out.

Some I knew, some I didn't but I knew they knew us and I was surprised they even tried their hand.

When we got to the backyard, there was a jumper for kids, a dice game, and even a game of dominoes going up. Taco Gyrl Catering was set up in the corner that Brook flew in from Cali and Brooklyn's uncle was on the grill flipping a slab of Ribs. The first person that spotted us was Breela.

"Cash!" she shouted, running towards me for a hug.

"Hey, sis," I smiled and hugged her back.

"I didn't think you were coming."

"I wasn't gonna come," I said, bashfully.

"I'm glad you did," she said giving me a side-eye that told me something wasn't right.

"Ugh!" I heard Nina say. I looked in the direction she was looking and noticed Carlos standing by the grill.

I scrunched my face up, puzzled because she looked like she didn't want to be bothered with him, which was shocking.

Let me find out, I thought to myself.

192

The moment Carlos spotted us, he looked at Nina and held her gaze. His eyes were pleading like he didn't know what to do, so he simply dropped his head.

"Bitch, what's up with yall?" I asked because last I heard, she was happy and in love.

"Girl, fuck him. I pulled up on him and some bitch was…" She stopped speaking because Carlos was now within arm's reach.

I stepped away a little to give them some privacy. I then began to scan the yard for Brooklyn but he wasn't nowhere in sight.

I wandered off into the home and the moment I opened the front door, a cloud of smoke hit me dead in the face, almost making me throw up. I put my hand over my mouth and nose to block the smell as I made my way through the home.

I walked down the long hallway in search for Brook, opening every door. Since it was Breela's home, I knew it like the back of my hand. I walked to the guest bedroom and reached to turn the nob but I was stopped in my tracks. I heard Brook's voice clear as day. He was shouting at the top of his lungs so I put my ear closer to the door to eavesdrop.

"So you have a cookout and not invite me, Nino?" I heard a female's voice.

"Man, I told you it was a surprise, Tiff."

The minute he said the name, Tiff my blood began to boil but I kept quiet and continued to listen in. They were shouting back and forth and from the sound of his voice, he sounded annoyed. Before I knew it the door flung open, Tiffany and I stood face to face. Her once angry face was now turned into a smirk. She then opened the door all the way so I could see inside. Brook was standing by the bed in only a towel that was wrapped tightly around his waist. He focused in on me and we locked eyes for what seemed like an eternity.

"I'm sorry," I whispered and turned around to leave.

"Cash!" He ran to the doorway, shouting my name but I kept straight.

Of course, he couldn't chase me because he was only wearing a towel, which was good for me because I didn't have shit to say to him. As bad as I wanted to cry, I held it in because I was now the cold-hearted bitch I was before.

When I made it outside, Nina was snuggled up under Carlos and they were both talking to Blaze who was standing with Tiny.

"Hey, Blaze. Hey, Tiny," I tried to sound like I was ok.

"I have to go, ma," I said to Nina, in a hurry.

"Awe, we just got here."

"I know. My mom is calling me. I'll probably come back, ok?"

"Ok," she said and that was my cue to leave before Brook came outside.

Brooklyn Nino

Fuck! I cursed myself tryna hurry and slide my clothes on to catch up with Cash. I felt like shit right now because she saw what I didn't want her to see.

"So you gon' just chase after the bitch?" Tiffany barked, five seconds from getting slapped.

"Watch yourself, Tiff!" I shot her a look that said I wasn't playing. "Matter fact, get the fuck on, yo!" I shook my head, annoyed.

Her eyes started watering but I didn't give two fucks about her tears. The moment she went to say another word, I shushed her up and she stormed out.

After I was totally dressed, I went outside, praying to god Cash was still here. I really wanted to holla at her because a nigga missed her like a muthafucka. I had finally talked to Carter and he ensured me they haven't fucked but no lie, I was still hurt over the kiss.

When I got to the back yard, I heard screaming so I ran to see what the fuck was going on. Nina was shouting at the top of her lungs and Tiffany was shouting right back at her. Out of nowhere, Tiny little ass clocked Tiff on the side of her head with a gun, dropping Tiff, instantly. Blaze snatched Tiny up and I ran to help Tiffany off the ground.

196

She was crying hysterical but that shit didn't change my mind one bit, I was still looking for Cash.

"Man, didn't I tell your ass to get the fuck on?"

"So it's like that, Nino?" she asked through tears.

"Man, just go!" I shouted and with one last look, she walked off.

"Where Cash at, y'all?" I asked but looking at Nina because I assumed that was who she had come with.

"Don't worry bout her now, Nino. She ain't fucking with you," Nina spoke with much attitude.

"It ain't even like that. This bitch Tiffany just popped up on a nigga."

"But you been fucking her, though, right?" Tiny asked. I guess the look I had told it all because everyone just got quiet.

"Look, Nino, I apologize," Nina said, sincerely. "Cash came to talk to you, so I suggest you go get your girl."

All I could do was shake my head.

197

I pulled out my phone and called Cash. To my surprise, she answered.

"Aye, ma, I swear, it ain't like that."

"It's cool, Brook. I mean we haven't been together in months so I expected you to move on," Cash said and that shit hurt like a knife.

"Where you at, I wanna holla at you?"

"I'm on my way to boo-up like you so I'll holla at you when I check out my hotel," and with that, she hung up.

I didn't know if I should believe her or not about booing-up because Cash was unpredictable. And, if it was one thing I knew for sure about her, she was a stone-cold player.

My blood was boiling and my heart was hurting, I prayed to God she wasn't giving up my pussy. Fuck That! I thought and shot her a text. If her ass didn't respond, I was going to find her.

Me: Cash, a nigga love you. Lil Mama, please don't do nothing stupid.

Lil Mama: Oh, like you been doing.

Me: I ain't been doing shit, ma.

Lil Mama: Nino, you cannot sit here and tell me you haven't fucked that girl since we've been broken up.

Me: Oh, so I'm Nino now?

Lil Mama: Exactly, I'll wait! was her last text.

I couldn't even lie to her because I knew that shit would only stir up more bullshit between us. I knew Cash like a book and if I had lied, all she would have done was popped up at the bitch Tiffany's door for assurance, and Tiffany would tell it all. Right then and there, I knew I had to cut Tiffany loose or I could lose Cash, for good.

I stormed back to my room heated. What was supposed to be a good day was turning out to be the worst.

"Knock, knock, knock," the sound of knocking pulled me from my train of thoughts. I really didn't feel like being bothered right now so I didn't even bother saying, come in.

Bronx walked in, willingly. I just looked up at him from my bed. He sighed and took a seat next to me.

199

"You straight, bro?"

"Yeah, I'm good, man. Shit just crazy."

"Yeah, I could only imagine," Bronx said while shaking his head. "Look, Nino, I'ma jump straight to the point. Have you ever loved someone but had to let go," he asked and looked at me.

Samantha, I mumbled to myself. "Hell yeah," I replied, thinking about my high school sweetheart. *To make a long story short, she left for college and I chose the streets. Of course, we knew what came with the streets (Hoes, jail and death).*

"Exactly! That's how I felt about Cash," he said, catching me off guard.

I looked over at him, wondering where this conversation was going but I let him continue.

"When I left, I had to leave Cash behind. She was the prettiest girl in the world to me, she was the best thing that ever happened to me, but I had to let her go. Even though I caught her ass with that nigga at the restaurant, I still wanted to repair what we had but it was too late. I couldn't risk you, Bree, my wife, and kids getting hurt over my dumb shit so I went out like Pac."

We both laughed.

"The day I left, my feelings went with me. I knew I had to forget about Cash and I did just that. Now, I am sorry for my frivolous acts with that kiss, I guess I was caught up in the heat of the moment. Gabriela sent that tape out of spite. Now I'm not blaming her because she acted off of emotions but I just wanna let you know from the horse's mouth. I apologize and I would never disrespect you again, on mama's. Me and Cash never fucked. It was a simple kiss that we ended quickly and we jumped straight on the plane here. The way Cash looks at you, the way her eyes light up when you're around, not to mention, her ass sick as fuck without you right now, that girl loves you, one hunnit. Once I seen it for myself, I couldn't do shit but fall back, Brooklyn. That's your life and soon to be wife, don't let her get away, bro. I know you might be feeling Tiffany, she seems like a sweet girl but is she worth losing Cash?"

"Hell nah she ain't, Bronx. I love Cash to death. I ain't gone lie, that kiss had a nigga heart shattered. I mean put yourself in my shoes, you get a random tape in the mail with yo girl kissing yo brother?" I said, shaking my head.

"I did put myself in your shoes. The day another man opened the door to my home, where my kids lay their heads and not to mention, making love to my wife. That shit

201

fucked me up. It made me realize, my wife is what I need in my life and I can't fuck this up for shit." Now he too was shaking his head.

"I feel you. Man, Cash ass stubborn."

"Nigga, she just reversed it on yo ass."

We both fell out laughing.

"Get yo girl, Nino!"

"I am. Shit, now I just gotta figure out a way."

"Nigga, Cash ol in love ass. All you gotta do is show up at her doorstep butt ass naked."

We laughed again.

"For real, though, bro. I love you and I'm happy you came to holla at me. Ah nigga feel a lot better."

"That's what's up."

He then stood up, pulled me by the arms so I could stand to my feet, then pulled me in for a hug. No lie, I felt a ton of bricks being lifted off my shoulders. Now, all I had to do was figure out how to get my wifey back but for now, we were about to go outside and turn the fuck up.

Chapter 15

Que

I pulled up to Nino's cookout at the ass end of everything. Nina had already sent me a text telling me what had happened with Nino and his little bitch Tiffany. I don't know why Nino didn't throw the hoe to me because clearly, he couldn't handle her and Cash at the same time. Hahaha, I laughed to myself because I was something else, But I was dead ass serious. Tiffany was fine than a muthafucka with a nice little frame, just the thought of what I would do to her sexy ass had a nigga dick hard.

I noticed everybody's whip out front, except Cash's. I then spotted the nigga Carter's whip but shrugged my shoulders. I knew I was risking it because he could expose me to his brother but fuck that nigga, I'll body both they ass. I had two beautiful ladies escorting me so I would be walking in like the nigga I was… a Boss. After we left the cookout, the lovely bitches would be joining me in my hot tub for some freaky sex and Hennessy. Tomorrow I had court, so I didn't know what I was up against, so tonight, I would go out with a bang. I knew that Ms. Lopez wouldn't let me down but playing with them fucking crackers, you never know.

When I walked in the gate, I was greeted by a fine ass little piece. Talk about love at first sight, this girl had a nigga mesmerized by not only her beauty but her whole swag. Damn! I thought to myself, eyeing shorty. She was about 5'6 with nice, long legs. Her skin was like an olive color and her big eyes were like a real doll. I'm a cocky nigga so I ran my hand through her hair to check for tracks and to my surprise, I didn't feel one lump.

"Ouch!" she shouted but smiled.

"I'm just checking, ma," I laughed. She gazed into my eyes as if she was feeling a nigga and the feelings were mutual. The smack of Kimberly's lips snapped me out my train of thoughts.

"Man, go make me a plate or something," I told Kim. I then looked at Ashanti with a look that said bye bitch, go with her.

When the two were out of ear distance, I began my macking.

"What's your name, ma?" I asked and she giggled shyly.

"Breela. And, yours?"

"I'm Quintin," I hit her with my government and extended my hand like a real gentleman.

"Why I never saw you before?"

"I don't know… I guess because I've been in college."

"College? Word?" Yeah, now I was really impressed.

"Man, get your ass away from my sister!" Nino shot, walking towards us.

"Oh, this your sister?" I threw my hands in the air in surrender.

Nino laughed and gave me a pound. I walked off but making sure I got one last look at Breela, and then made my way to the backyard.

When I got to the back, I greeted Nina, Blaze, and Tiny, not saying shit to Carter as he mugged me. My bitches walked up on me and handed me a plate and then stood by my side.

"You wild, boy," Blaze said, laughing, causing Nina and Tiny to laugh with him.

After making small talk, I walked over to the bar that Nino had set up and got me and my bitches a drank to start our night.

***

I woke up the next morning with a slight hangover. When I looked over at my nightstand, it was almost 9:30. Shit! I cursed myself because I was going to be late. I stayed up all night getting fucked and sucked by Kim and Ashanti but for some reason, I couldn't get Breela off my mind. This shit was crazy because I had never though about any woman this much, other than Cash. I had to suck it up and accept that Cash would be with Nino, forever, so I had to live my life. I just prayed it would be with Ms. Breela's sexy ass.

"Aye, yall bitches gotta go!" I said, waking them up to leave.

They didn't even put up a fight. They simply got up and threw their last night's garments on and left without another word.

I hurried and jumped in the shower, and then slid my clothes on. I rocked a three-piece Armani suit so I could look halfway square, however, I knew it wouldn't work because of my tattoos that adorned my entire body.

When I hopped in the car, I threw in my Rick Ross CD and jumped on the highway in faith that Ms. Lopez and Diane made this situation go away. Once I picked Diane up from her condo out in Bay Shore, we hopped back on the highway towards the courtroom.

The moment we walked into the courtroom, I took a seat behind the bailiff. As soon as I looked up at the judge, my mind drifted to my daughter. Man, I couldn't see myself gone out of her life for all that time they were trying to give me. The max was sixty years, therefore, I'd never see daylight again. I then thought about Breela. Damn, I ain't gon never be able to hit that pussy, I thought to myself, wishing I could walk back out these doors and go on a run.

When the judge called my name, I proceeded to the podium and stood by my lawyer, Diane.

"Your honor, I ask that all charges be dropped against my client," Diane spoke with force.

The judge looked from Diane to me, and then he looked at the papers in his hand.

"I object, your honor. We have the transcripts of the informant, clearly stating the defendant sold him 26 kilos of drugs," The DA said, annoyed.

"Your honor, transcripts aren't enough to hold my client in custody."

"The hell they aren't. Your client is a known drug dealer and not to mention, an ex-con."

"That's still not enough to hold my client," Diane shot at the DA, now sounding annoyed.

"Your honor, there's evidence that could convict the defendant."

"Bring the evidence forward," the judge said, and waited for the DA to present the evidence.

The detective then whispered over to the DA and said something to him that no one could hear. Right then, the DA slammed his hands on the table in front of him.

"You gotta be shitting me!" the DA shouted throughout the courtroom.

I looked at Diane and she had a smirk on her face like she knew exactly what happened to the evidence.

"Your honor, do you see that all this was made up against my client. He has been stopped several times by the same officers. Then, his home was raided and they found nothing. Every time they harass my client, they find nothing."

The judge looked up again from the DA to Diane.

"I have nothing further, your honor," Diane said, then took a seat next to me.

"I have no further questions, your honor," the DA said, and cursed himself, quietly.

The judge didn't wait no time as he banged his gavel. "This case is dismissed!" he shouted and left his seat, heading through the wooden door.

These muthafuckas didn't have to tell me twice. I jumped to my feet and met with Diane outside the courtroom. We hopped on the elevator but making sure we didn't say anything. When we got to the car, I told her she was driving and we quickly hopped in like the judge could change his mind.

"Man, thank you, ma," I said, reaching over to peck her on the cheek. I then reached into my pocket and pulled out the thirty bands I planned on giving her.

"You're welcome, Que, and you are family, man, you don't have to give me anything. Plus, Ms. Lopez gave me a hundred thousand as a thank you. I told her she didn't have to give me anything because you guys are family, but she insisted."

"Same as me, ma. Just take the money because if you don't, I'll just leave it in your house," I laughed, sitting the money down on her armrest.

She smiled and just looked at me.

Diane then pulled up not too far from the courthouse. I was puzzled to why were we here but I was so happy to be a free man, shit, Diane could kidnap a nigga all day.

A car pulled up on the side of us and Diane was smiling from ear to ear. She got out the car and strutted over to the other car with that sexy ass walk she had. When I looked towards the ride, I was shocked as shit as the DA exited the car and popped Diane on her ass. I couldn't help but laugh as I laid my seat back and pulled out my phone to post on Facebook.

Search: Breela Carter

I typed in her name. I felt like a real stalker, but oh well. Baby girl was my future and she didn't even know it yet, but she would soon find out. Bingo! I found her sexy ass. In her profile picture, she rocked a sweatshirt that read Howard University. I was really in love now, I just prayed she would accept my request.

After Diane talked to the DA for a while, he got in his car but making sure to hit me with a thumbs up before he sat in his seat. Diane then walked to my window and I already knew what that meant.

"Bye, Que," she said, giggling and causing me to laugh.

"A'ight, ma. And a do me a favor."

"What's that?"

"Suck that nigga dick till his shit pink," I laughed and she playfully hit me on the shoulder. She then strutted off, switching her little booty so I got over to the driver side and pulled off.

When I made it home, I laid in bed and drifted off into deep thought. I was a free fucking man and it felt good. I then pulled out my phone to see if Breela accepted my request. To my surprise, she did. I was smiling from ear to ear as I posted my first status.

What's on your mind?

I'm a Free Man!

Then I posted my second status.

My little college shorty been on my mind all night.
#B

Ten minutes later Breela posted…

What's on your mind?

Baby had my full attention (smiley face)

Que…

What's on your mind?

I don't know if she can handle a nigga like me.

Breela…

What's on your mind?

I'm a big girl (smiley face).

After going back and forth, I shot her an inbox. I was tired of playing the cat and mouse game, even though it was kind of cute.

Messenger: What's up, ma. How's your day going?

Messenger: It's going pretty good. How about yours?

Messenger: Shit, so far so good. But even better now since I'm talking to you.

I massaged her right when my phone started ringing. Shit! I cursed because me and Breela's massages were being interrupted.

"Yeah," I answered, annoyed.

214

"Damn, what's wrong with you?" Stephanie said into the phone.

"Nothing, what's up?"

"I'm outside, come open the door," she said.

I looked at my phone, and again, I cursed.

I got up to open the door and let her ass in. No lie, she was looking good as fuck so I let her ass right in. I couldn't get Breela's pretty ass so fuck it, I settled for this warm pussy from Steph.

Chapter 16

Cash

I was mad at myself because here I was, pregnant, and couldn't move on with my life. As bad as I wanted to call Quan, I couldn't bring myself to sleep with someone because of this baby growing inside of me. I needed some dick in a major way.

Fuck it! I thought as I slid into my clothes. Today, I was going to head to the mall and then my shop so I could busy myself and not stress off Brooklyn. Tomorrow was the big day for Nina and Carlos. It was the day of their baby shower and the sex of their baby will be revealed. Once I was fully dressed, I headed out the door for a day of shopping.

Once I made it to the mall, I went straight to the Gucci Store and bought the baby some Gucci shoes that were unisex. I stopped in a few stores and picked up a few items for me, and even grabbed my mother a few things. After I was done, I headed to my jeweler so I could buy the baby some diamond studs, I bought two just in case it was a girl. I also bought a bracelet that was 10 karats and then made my way back to my car.

When I pulled up to the shop, it was busy as hell, which was typical for a Friday. There were men sitting in every seat, a few guys over by the pool table and a few waiting to be seen. I went straight to my office so I could take a seat because I was feeling some nausea. After trying to gather myself, I noticed on my surveillance that Monique was headed in so I stood to my feet prepared for whatever it was she wanted. Since I been back, Monique and I haven't said too much to each other so I was puzzled that she would even try and come talk to me.

"What's up, Mo?" I asked the moment she stepped in.

"Hey, Cash," she said, walking over to take a seat.

"Chilling, pretty much. I see yall busy as hell today."

"Hell yeah. I can't even get a break."

"Get that money," I said, causing her to smile. She was fidgeting in her seat so I knew she had something to say.

"I wanted to tell you. I ran into Tiffany. The girl…"

"Yeah, I knew who she is."

"Yeah, well, her. She's telling everybody that she's been messing with Nino and they were together now."

"Yeah, I've heard that. But check it, I'm not worried bout her or Nino. To be honest, she could have him," I said and began scrolling through my phone.

"Oh, ok. Well, I thought I'd let you know," Mo said and got up from her seat. The smirk that she wore let me know she was indeed trying to rub it in my face, therefore, I had to act nonchalant like it didn't bother me one bit.

The moment she left my office, I laid back on the couch and tried my hardest to contain my anger…

***

Nina's baby shower was in full effect. The decorator did a great job with the pink and blue theme. She had a catering company come out and cater along with a bar and a hired bartender. There were twenty huge tents set up and about five tables under each tent. I spotted my table that had a reserved sign that read Nino and Cash. This bitch thinks she slick. I smirked and turned around to go find her, but ran into Lydia and Carter. She gave an uneasy look and walked to a table to take a seat.

"Hey, Carter," I waved and he pulled me in for a hug. The look on Lydia's face told it all. The bitch hated me now, thanks to the Brazilian bimbo, for sending her that tape. I made a mental note to have a one-on-one with Lydia, but I would wait until another day, just in case things got heated.

"Cash!" Diane shouted, walking in with Niya.

"Hey, bitches!" I shouted and gave them both a hug.

We walked over to the table that read My Divas so I could show them that this is where they would be sitting. Knowing my girls, they weren't going to be sitting, they were going to head for the bar, and I would be joining them.

219

When we made it to the bar, I was jealous because I couldn't order my usual Hennessy so I had to settle with a glass of wine. The moment the tender gave us our glasses, Nina came out the house, shouting.

"Hell no, Cash! That better not be alcohol!" she said, causing us to look up.

"Ugh, fall back, hoe!" I said and turned my head back towards the bar.

"Nope, I'm not falling back, hoe! You know you ain't supposed to be drinking!" she was shouting.

When I turned to curse her out, Brook and I locked eyes. He was standing there with a puzzled look, curious to why I couldn't drink. He then looked down at my stomach like he was trying to see if I was indeed pregnant. I was only a few months I could basically hide my pudge in anything. I stormed off, away from the girls because I didn't want to hear shit Brook had to say.

I walked in the house to hide my embarrassment. To be honest, I contemplated having an abortion but now that Nina's big mouth ass said what she said, I was more than sure Brook would confront me any minute. I ran into the kitchen for a bottled water when I was stopped in my tracks. Que looked up at me like he knew he was caught and Breela stood off to the side, trying to hide her smile.

"What yall ass in here doing?" I asked, looking from Que to Bree, back to Que. It wasn't my business so I quickly grabbed the bottled water and left as fast as I had come.

Carter gone kill Que, I laughed to myself.

When I got back outside, Brooklyn was sitting at my table. Nina was smirking at me as she sat with the girls, instead of her table that was for her and Carlos. I went and took a seat at the table with my mother and Esco, and stuck my tongue out at the girls in the process of me sitting down. They were laughing as Nina shouted, "That's not your table!" My mother was laughing hysterically but the look on Esco's face said something was up.

"Cash, do you know that young lady sitting over there?" Esco said, pointing to the table about two tables down.

"I think she came with Que. It looks like the same woman I had seen at his house the other night."

221

"She looks very familiar, I can't quite put my hand on it," Esco said, but not taking his eyes off the lady.

Que is crazy, I laughed to myself. Here he was, creeping in the kitchen with Breela, and he had company with him.

Tiny and Blaze walked in hand and hand so I jumped up to hug the two. I then walked over to the table that read My Boyz, which was Blaze and Que's table. I grabbed Tiny's hand as soon as she tried to sit down and walked her over to the Diva table.

Carlos walked up on us and handed me an envelope that I assumed was the sex of the baby. Nina took the floor and asked for everybody's attention so I took it as my Que to walk over. Once Nina had everyone's attention, she then explained I would be revealing the baby's sex.

As I stood there about to read the card, I could feel Brooklyn's eyes watching me. I dropped my head and opened the envelope, Nina, and Carlos who were patiently waiting to know.

"It's a Girl!" I shouted.

Carlos had a huge grin, but Nina smacked her lips.

Everybody ran to her and started hugging and congratulating her. Breela walked up and handed everyone a roll of tissue so we could start our first game. Little did everybody know, me and Nina had already cheated so I pulled off the eleven squares of tissue.

I sat patiently and waited as everyone pulled their tissue squares off the roll. All of a sudden, I felt nausea so I quickly jumped to my feet and ran in the house to the restroom. I dropped to my knees and began throwing up everything I had eaten. I didn't know if it was the liquor or what, but this baby wasn't having it. After finally regaining myself, I rinsed my mouth with mouthwash and then headed for the door. As soon as I opened it, Brooklyn stood there with a grin. I tried to walk past him, but he grabbed my arms and stopped me.

"So, you pregnant?" he asked.

I just looked at him ready to lie, but I knew I was caught dead bang. "Do it matter? You've moved on, Brooklyn."

"What the fuck you mean do it matter. ma? Hell yeah, it matters. Then you drinking and shit!"

"I'm fine, man!"

223

"Shit, it don't look like it to me," he said, looking angry.

"I'm fine!"

"You not getting rid of my baby if that's what you think, Cash."

"I'm not about to bring a baby into this world as a single parent, Nino."

"You not single! And don't call me that!"

"Oh, I'm very much single."

"Stop playing with me, Cash! You're my woman and after this shower, we're going home so we can talk," he shouted and stormed out, heading back outside.

When I walked back out, everyone was in their seats, waiting for the winner to be announced. Breela stood in front of all the tents with a pad and pencil in her hand, ready to announce the winner.

"Cash! You're the winner!" she announced.

I stood up and walked over to where she stood. We have one more winner! She shouted and looked at me with a smirk.

224

"Brooklyn!" she announced with a grin.

I snatched both the strips of tissue out her hand and began counting each square. I'd be damned Brooklyn's ass had won with me.

He walked over to us smiling from ear to ear and grabbed his gift. He then walked up on me and kissed me but laughing at the same time. "I'm a winner, baby," he whispered in my ear and I couldn't help but smile.

Everyone was laughing at us as he led me to the table that was reserved for the both of us.

When I looked up, Nina ol emotional ass had a single tear running down her face. She was watching me and Brook while crying and smiling at the same damn time.

Looking around the yard, it was like I was the most hated. Lydia was throwing daggers at me with her eyes and even Que's little boo was smirking at me. These bitches are buggin, I thought to myself and then focused in on Que.

He was eye-fucking Breela from across the room so I quickly turned my head, not to alarm Brooklyn who was grilling me. I smiled widely because I knew I was getting some dick tonight. I sat back, feeling good and enjoyed the rest of the shower.

Chapter 17

Brooklyn Nino

Finally, the baby shower was over, I was ready to get home and relax with Cash. I made her leave her ride at Nina's house because I couldn't take a chance with her stubborn ass. A nigga couldn't stop smiling at the thought of Cash finally having my baby so, at this point, I would do anything to repair our relationship. To be honest, I figured she was pregnant because I had been sick and sleeping a lot. Once Cash had admitted it was her that was pregnant, I was relieved that it wasn't Tiffany. I didn't want to ask Tiff because she was the type of chick that would have said yes, and then faked a miscarriage on a nigga so I left it alone.

The car ride home was so quiet that all I could hear was the clicking of Cash's phone. When I pulled through my security gates, I parked right in the front of the door. Cash didn't waste any time going inside. On the ride here, she looked exhausted like she had a long day. I wanted to leave her in peace, but we needed to talk. I hated she had to see me and Tiff together so I needed her to understand that Tiffany was just something to do.

Cash went straight to the shower as I slid into some b-ball shorts and relaxed on the bed, in deep thought. Once she was done, she went into my drawer, pulled out one of my oversized t-shirts and slid it on with nothing under it. Just the sight of her sexy ass had my dick rock hard, causing a tent in my shorts. Damn, I missed my baby!

"Come here, Lil Mama, lemme holla at you," I told her and she did just that.

The moment she laid beside me, I gazed into her eyes and began my plea.

"Look, ma. I hate you had to see what you saw the other day. On my mama, I didn't invite the bitch to my cookout. Now I'm not gone sit here and lie and say I wasn't fucking with her because I was. I'ma be straight up with you, I was so mad at you, I just knew I wasn't going to be with you anymore so I started fucking with her. My brother reached out to me and swore that nothing happened between yall, other than that kiss. Now I could be fooled but I believed him."

228

"Do you love her, Brooklyn?"

"Hell no! That bitch don't mean shit to me."

"So, why is it her that you keep running back to?" Cash asked, eyeing me with so much hurt in her eyes.

"To be honest, because a nigga ain't got time to be out here searching for a new bitch. Tiffany ain't shit but rebound pussy that I know whenever I call, she gonna come running. I don't have no types of feeling for her, whatsoever. You the only woman that hold a nigga's heart."

"I don't think I could trust you with her. I mean, how would I know you and the bitch won't be creeping behind my back?"

"For one, you're everything I need in one. Ain't no bitch worth me creeping with and losing you. These hoes can't stand next to you, Cash, and I've told you that before."

The moment I said it she dropped her head. I lifted her chin to look at me and her eyes had tears in them that hurt a nigga's heart. No lie, I hated seeing Cash cry. That's the only thing on this earth that hurt a nigga the most.

"I'm sorry, Brook," she said, above a whisper.

"It's ok, ma. I forgive you. But I swear, Cash, if anything ever happened between you and my brother, I'ma body both yall," I said and meant every word.

Cash didn't even bother to respond so I changed the subject.

"So I'm bout to be a daddy? I said, smiling widely.

"Yes," Cash finally spoke, eyes wide. She started smiling and that shit felt good to see her happy.

"Nino Jr.?"

"Nope sorry, I'm having a girl."

"How you know?"

"I don't know, I could just feel it," she said, and we both laughed.

I pulled her close to me and kissed her like it would be our last. The inside of me felt good just to have my baby back and this time, I wasn't letting her get away. I flipped her ass on top me because it was time I relieved the tension I had built up inside of me. Even though I had smashed Tiffany a few times, it wasn't no pussy like Cash's pussy, so I prepared myself for the best.

230

***

As soon as I opened my eyes, I looked over at Cash who was still peacefully sleeping. I went downstairs to make us some breakfast so that I could serve her breakfast in bed. Today, I wanted to pamper her by giving her a massage from head to toe and then take her out later to find a wedding dress. My phone began ringing so I snatched it up without looking.

"I thought you were coming over last night, Nino?" Tiffany shouted.

Shit! I cursed myself, mad I hadn't looked at the phone first.

"I got caught up…"

"Nah, you were at that baby shower so I'm guessing you and your boo hooked back up."

"Well, since you know so much, why are you asking?"

"Just tell me, Nino!"

"Honestly, yes, Tiffany. You know what it is with me and Cash, so why you acting puzzled?"

"Well look, just stop playing with my emotions. You keep running back to me like I'm a rebound bitch. Just stay away from me, Nino!" Tiffany shouted and then began crying.

"Man, stop crying, Tiff. I'm sorry if you feel I lead you on, but Cash is my wife."

"So, fuck me, huh? It's crazy because I was here before Cash and you shit on me. I'm tired of playing second best! Bye, Nino, I won't disturb your life anymore," she said and with that, she hung up.

For the first time, Tiffany had a nigga feeling bad. But fuck that, I couldn't fall for that guilt trip because she knew the deal with me and Cash. I just shook my head and headed upstairs to Cash with breakfast in my hands.

Her ass was knocked out, mouth open, and slightly snoring. I stood back and admired her for a minute. She was the most beautiful creature, even with the little bit of drool hanging from her lips. Cash reminded me of Ariel from The Little Mermaid. Her big pretty eyes and small lips. I couldn't stand that movie growing up because Breela

232

watched it over and over, and every time I would tell my mother, she'd simply say, "Leave that child alone, go outside and play with your brother." So I'd be stuck watching that shit a million times. No lie, Ariel fine ass grew on me so every time Bree watched it, I'd watch it with her.

"Cash," I called her name and shook her slightly.

"Huh, umm yes, Brook," she said, seductive like she was dreaming a nigga was dicking her down or something.

"Cash, wake up, ma," I shook her again and finally, her eyes opened. She looked at me strangely, and then lifted up, rubbing her eyes.

"Damn, Brook, I was just about to bust my nut," she said, and we both laughed.

"I'm right here, baby. Why are you having dreams and shit? Eat, so I could give you this soul pole, ma," I said, and again, we both laughed.

"Well, fuck this food," she said, playfully pushing away the tray.

"Yeah right, ma. Yo fat ass ain't bout to let me take that plate from you."

"Shol ain't!" she said, smiling.

"Aye, ma, check it. After you eat, I wanna rub you down. After, I wanna take you shopping for your wedding dress," I said and she stopped in her tracks.

"Are you serious?" she asked. Her eyes lit up like a four-year-old going to Toys R Us.

"Yeah, I'm serious. It's about that time."

She then shoved the food from in front of her and hugged me tightly.

Damn, I won't be getting no pussy, I thought to myself.

"Awww, I love you, Nino," she said, jumping up from the bed and heading to the restroom. I followed behind her and began my normal routine.

"So, you know what day you wanna get married?"

"Um yes, I guess, December 23rd."

"Ok, but why that day?" I asked, puzzled.

234

"It's my Abuela's birthday."

Again, I looked puzzled.

"My grandma, fool," she laughed.

"Ok, December 23rd it is," I said, which was three months away. Shit to be truthful, we could have got married today, but I had to give my baby what she wanted.

"Yayyyy!" she shouted and ran up to me with her arms extended.

I took it as my cue. I gave her a hug, slickly, and then sat her thick ass on the counter top. I pulled her shirt over her head and flung it across the bathroom. I spread her legs widely and went head first into her pussy, causing her to jump with each flick of my tongue. When she finally relaxed, I went in like it was the last meal on earth.

After causing her to have an orgasm, my dick was rock hard and ready to perform. I slid the head into her opening and to keep from shouting like a hoe, I bit my lip instead. Her pussy was so fucking warm and tight, I knew right then and there, it hadn't been tampered with. I started hitting her with long deep strokes. Her ass was screaming like I was killing her, I just prayed I wasn't.

"I'm not hurting you, am I?" I asked while stroking her slowly.

"Kinda. But I'm ok."

I tried to ease up but I couldn't help myself. I needed to feel every part of her insides.

"Ahhh, shit, Brooklyn!"

"You Ms. Daddy dick, huh?"

"Yes! Oh my God, yes, daddy."

"Oh, I could tell," I said and slid out, looking at my dick. It was covered in white cream from the multiple nuts Cash was busting.

"I love you, Nino! Oh shit, I love you, Big Poppa!"

Damn, she ain't called me that in forever, I must be hitting it right, I thought to myself.

I then began speeding up my pace. I then quickly pulled out because I felt myself about to bust. I pulled Cash by her arms and led her to the toilet. I took a seat and she knew exactly what it meant.

"Ride this muthafucka."

236

She climbed on top of me, but with her back facing me. She then slid me inside of her and when I was fully entered, she bent over so that her hands could use the floor for support. She slowly began to grind her hips. Before I knew it, she was throwing her ass up and down, without moving the rest of her body. Her pregnant ass was throwing that shit, therefore, I knew at any moment, I would be busting.

"Ride yo dick, baby!"

"Oooh! It feels good, daddy?"

"Hell yeah, ma. This the best pussy on earth."

"Oooh, shit. I'm about to cum, baby!"

"Cum then, ma. Let it go!"

"Ahhhhh, shit!" she shouted, and it felt like a gush of water poured from her pussy. That shit felt so good, I burst right behind her.

"Ahrrrrr!" My legs were shaking as I emptied every last drop inside of her.

She lifted up off me and went to the bed to collapse. I followed right behind her and collapsed on the side of her.

We both were trying to catch our breath and before I knew it, we had dozed off for a much-needed nap.

Chapter 18

Cash

3 months later...

We were one week away from the wedding and I was extremely excited. I had just come back from getting the final touches on my dress so that it would fit, my now, huge stomach. I was almost six months pregnant so I waited to near the date to have the back of my dress stitched to my size. Brooklyn and I found out the sex of the baby at my last appointment. Brooklyn was happy because his dreams of having a Jr. had come true.

"I'm so excited!" Nina squealed, causing me to laugh.

"Ugh, you're next, hoe," Niya said, looking at Nina.

"Girl, I'm not getting married no time soon," Nina shot back.

Niya then looked down at her phone, then looked back up smiling.

"Oh, Ms. Thang, who got you over there smiling?"

Before Niya could reply, Nina spoke up.

"Her little college boo."

"Shut up hoe, dang," Niya said, still smiling.

"Speaking of, how you doing in school?" I asked Niya who was still looking like she was on cloud nine.

"It's going great. I'll be finally done in two weeks then I take my state boards."

"Yay! That's what's up," I cheered her on.

"Ooh shit, yall," Nina said in a panic, and Niya and I looked over at her.

Then, out of nowhere, it looked like she was peeing on herself.

"Nina!" Niya shouted, also in a frantic.

240

"I think my water just broke," Nina began to cry.

The entire time we been out, Nina had complained about pain. Every time we asked her was she ok, she would simply say, "I'm fine."

"Come on, we gotta get her to the hospital!" I grabbed one arm, Niya grabbed the other, and we rushed her out the store towards the car.

"Ahh, shit!" She bent down, grabbing her stomach.

We stopped to coach her, figuring it was a contraction.

"Niya, time her contractions, ma," I told Niya and she pulled out her phone.

"Ohh my God, yall, it hurts!" Nina cried harder.

I took Nina's phone from her hand and shot Carlos a text to meet us at the hospital. I then text Brook and then Blaze and Tiny.

When we finally got her to the car, I threw Niya the keys then jumped in the back seat with Nina. I watched the clock closely and her contractions were now three minutes apart.

"Hurry, Niya, hurry!"

"I'm trying to, these fucking cars are driving like dick heads!"

"Ahhhhh!" Nina cried out.

"Breathe, ma, breathe!" I tried coaching her. No lie, this shit was scary and I was now unprepared for the birth of my baby.

After about 15 minutes of driving, we were pulling into Miami Memorial Hospital. We hopped out and hurried in. Nina was placed into a wheelchair and took upstairs to labor and delivery. They took her into a room and told us that they would keep us informed. Carlos came in looking worried then followed by Brooklyn. A nurse came from inside the room and told us that they would be admitting her because she was four centimeters. Carlos went inside the room with Nina so I took a seat next to Brooklyn.

The doors came flying open and Que walked in. I looked over at Brooklyn to see his reaction because Breela was following closely behind him.

Oh shit! I thought to myself and when I looked over at Brook, his once sincere facial expression was now replaced with a grimace look. He jumped to his feet, looking from Bree to Que, back to Bree.

"I know yall not on no bullshit!"

"Nah, Nino, it ain't nothing like that."

"Then tell me what it is because from what it looks like, you done macked in on my fucking sister."

"Last I checked, I was grown, Brooklyn! I'm tired of yall treating me like a child," Bree protested.

"It's not about treating you like a child, It's about protecting you from niggas like this," Brook said, pointing to Que.

"Man, what's that supposed to mean?" Que spoke.

"Que, you know damn well you ain't shit, my nigga. My little sister not some fucking rag doll for you to play with."

"All I did was gave her a ride, though, Nino, damn. You act like a nigga bout to marry shorty tomorrow or something," Que said, right then, the doctor came into the waiting room to inform us that the godparents can go into the room at the time of delivery.

I grabbed Brook's arm to pull him away. Before he turned to walk away, he shot Que a cold look then proceeded to the back.

Brooklyn Nino

I was so fucking livid, I couldn't even focus on Nina having her baby. All I could hear is "Pushhhhhh!" My mouth moved to help coach, but my mind was a million miles away.

I couldn't say I didn't blame Que because my little sister was gorgeous, but damn, yo, that's a nigga little fucking sister, and Que was too much for her. Breela had her head on straight, and I didn't need her being knocked off focus behind a nigga like Que. Just the thought of that nigga trying to fuck on my little sis had me ready to body his ass, and I knew if Carter found out, shit would be even worse.

The sound of a baby knocked my thoughts back. I quickly ran to Cash's side and watched our God daughter as the doctors cleaned her up. The shit with Bree and Que could wait because right now, I was pumped up and couldn't wait for my son to be born.

After finally being able to snatch Cash away from the baby, we headed home. The car ride was silent as fuck, I was so in deep thought, I almost missed our exit. Cash watched me closely. She looked like she had so much to say but she remained quiet because she knew nothing could change how I felt.

When we made inside the house, I went straight to the room and slid into something comfortable. I laid down with the remote in my hand and listened to Cash babble about how cute Nina's baby was. To be honest, that shit went through one ear and out the other.

"Brook, do you hear me?" Cash asked, and fucked my whole train of thought up.

"Huh? Yeah, ma, I heard you."

"Well, what did I just say?" she asked with her face frowned up.

"Honestly, I don't even know, ma."

"Look! I understand you're upset about Breela and Que but, bae, Breela is grown so she's gonna do what she wants."

"Man, fuck all that! That nigga ain't bout to be fucking with my sister," I said, annoyed.

"Then, guess what they'll just sneak behind your back. You know what it's like when you like someone and, to be honest, they seem like they really like each other."

"Cash, I'm not about to…" I tried to speak, but I was cut short because Cash had snatched my briefs off and stuck my entire dick in her mouth. She knew exactly how to shut a nigga up.

She twirled her tongue around the head of my wood. She got it nice and wet and then swallowed it whole. I grabbed the back of her head and guided her up and down to satisfy my likings. She moaned out loud like I was hitting the pussy. The more noise she made, the harder my dick got, I could feel it growing in her mouth. I threw my hands behind my head and closed my eyes.

This was about to be a nigga wifey, was my last thoughts before I was in pure ecstasy.

Bronx Carter

"So, you're gonna go to a bitch wedding you been fucking all along?" Lydia shouted at me at the top of her lungs.

"Man, I ain't being fucking her, ma."

"But you have fucked her!"

"Man, why the fuck you tripping! She's with my brother now, Lydia!"

"What the fuck you mean why I'm tripping? You were fucking her before you faked your death," Lydia shot at me.

I gave her a puzzled looked before speaking. "What the fuck are you talking about?"

"Yeah, you didn't know I knew! She was the same bitch at your fake ass funeral. I knew the bitch looked familiar. Then, Brook brought her to my home, to my fucking daughter's party! That hoe knew exactly what she was doing. I bet she knew you were alive the whole time."

"I wasn't fucking with you then, so why the fuck does it matter!" I yelled, causing her to jump.

"So I guess you and your brother like sharing bitches," she mumbled under her breath.

"You know what? I'm finna roll, man before I fuck around and put my hands on you!"

I was five seconds from backhanding Lydia's ass so I just slid my clothes on and left my house. I was tired of her nagging about Cash. Yes, I fucked with Cash but so what, Lydia and I weren't together. I admit, I fucked up when I kissed her but so fucking what, this bitch had a nigga living in my house and around my fucking kids.

The sound of my phone ringing knocked my thoughts back. When I looked at the caller ID, it was Nino so I quickly answered.

"Sup, bro?" I answered and I knew I sounded stressed out.

"Damn, what's wrong with you?"

"Man, Lydia's ass," I said, shaking my head like he could see me.

"What she tripping on now?"

"Man, some bullshit, really," I lied. My brother and Cash's wedding day was tomorrow and I didn't want to spark up unnecessary drama, so I just kept the shit to myself.

"Man, I got something I wanna holla at you about."

"What's up?" I asked, anxious.

"I'ma wait till after the wedding, though. Shit gon' get ugly and I don't need shit fucking up Cash's day."

"Yeah, I feel you."

"So, where you headed at this time of night?"

"To be honest, I don't even know," I sighed out of frustration.

"Well, if you need to come here, you know my door is always open."

"Fasho, I'ma hit you if I need to come crash."

Chapter 19

Que

I was getting dougie to head to Cash and Nino's wedding. I had finally convinced Breela to roll with me and to my surprise, she agreed. After an entire day of shopping, we were now in my home, ready to face what was ahead for us. I knew her brothers would trip but so fucking what. I was feeling Breela in a real way and nobody was going to come between that.

After Nina's baby shower, I dropped Stephanie off and picked up Breela. I took her to the beach and the little innocent girl her brothers thought she was bullshit because she gave up the draws that same night. I could've played Breela like a little thot but I could tell she was feeling the kid in a major way, so I gave her a chance.

Breela and I were still getting to know each other and so far, I loved every piece of her. No lie, I had shit

251

going on in my life with these other bitches, but as far as I was concerned, fuck them. She was the kind of girl I could really see myself with so I would do everything in my power to make her fall in love with me. I didn't know how Breela would feel about me having a baby on the way, I just prayed she wouldn't up and stop fucking with a nigga.

I had just spent a good ten bands on Bree and watching her pretty ass twirl in my mirror, she was worth every penny. No lie, baby girl was looking bad as fuck in her ballroom gown. Shit, if I didn't know any better, I would have thought she was the one getting hitched.

"You look pretty, baby girl," I told her, looking her up and down but stopping at her titties.

"Thank you," she squealed and came over to kiss me.

"Girl, you betta watch out before we be skipping this wedding," I said and she laughed shyly.

"You're not tired of me yet, Quintin?" she asked, calling me by my government. The way she said it alone, had my dick rock hard.

"I could never get tired of you, ma. Honestly, I want you forever."

"Awww, you mean it?"

"Yep, every bit of it. I'm really feeling you, Bree, and I'll take my chances to make you mine,"

I said, referring to her brothers.

She didn't say anything else, she simply sashayed over to a nigga and kissed me like we just said I DO!

***

I ain't gone lie, I tapped that ass before we walked out the door. Breela was teasing a nigga and I couldn't help myself, so we got a quickie in and headed out so we wouldn't be later than we already were. I couldn't believe I was about to say this or was it because of Bree, but I was happy for Cash and Nino. I would always love Cash to death but I had to give her away. Since her and Nino had been together, she put that man through hell and back so he deserved my bitch. Yeah, you heard right... My Bitch.

"Why you so quiet?" Breela asked, knocking my thoughts back. I looked at her, not knowing what to say because I couldn't tell her I was thinking bout Cash, so I simply lied.

"I'm thinking bout how fire my pussy was just now."

She looked at me and smiled.

"Your pussy?"

"Yeah, my pussy, baby girl. You belong to me now and I swear if you give my loving to anybody, both yall gone be getting buried right next to each other."

She just looked at me and didn't say a word. It looked as if she was gathering her thoughts and about to speak up but her phone rung and sidetracked her.

"Hello?"

"So this the little bitch Que's been sniffing up under?"

"What? Who is this?"

"Don't worry about it, Ms. Breela! Just know that I know all about you."

254

"Look bitch, I ain't got time to be playing games with you."

"Oh, don't worry about me, you worry bout the nigga you in the car with. Why yall so busy playing house, did he tell you he's the one that tried to kill Carter and that's why Carter faked his death?"

"What!" I heard Bree say like something was wrong.

"What's wrong, ma?" I asked, getting worried.

"Oh my God!" Bree looked at me with tears in her eyes, then lifted back in her seat like she wanted to get away from me.

"Man, who the fuck is that, Bree?" I asked, curious to why she was now crying after her phone call.

I pulled over on the side of the road and tried to calm her down because she was now crying uncontrollably. When the car came to a complete stop, she reached for the door but it was locked.

"Man, Breela! What the fuck…" I yelled but I was caught dead in my tracks at the sound of gunfire.

255

Bock! Bock! Bock! Bock! Bock! Bock! Bock! Bock! Bock! Bock! Bock! Bock! Bock! Bock! Bock! Bock! Bock! Bock! Bock! Bock! Bock! Bock! Bock! Bock! Bock! Bock! Bock! Bock! Bock! Bock! Bock! Bock! Bock! Bock! Bock! Bock! Bock! Bock! Bock! Bock! Bock! Bock! Bock! Bock!

I felt a stinging sensation in my leg then my neck. I tried to move my head in search for Breela but the pain was too unbearable. With all my might, I forced myself to look into my passenger seat and Breela was hunched over. I then focused in on the blood that was quickly filling the front of her dress. I shook my head repeatedly, knowing my life was over.

Shit!

All the dirt, all the drama, all the hearts I broke, my karma had finally caught up to me. I never thought I'd see the day that I would get caught slipping but I guess my time was now. I knew exactly who was behind this shit; the fucking Carlito's. I knew, sooner or later, they would have come for me because I didn't deliver the promise. It was one thing with those Mexican muthafuckas, if the job didn't get done, then you would become the job. I couldn't even cry, though. I was that nigga Que, a true fucking soldier.

All I could do was say a silent prayer for Bree, for my kids, and for Cash. I simply closed my eyes and waited for my maker to come get me.

Blaze and Tiny

"Bae, you almost ready?" I shouted upstairs to Tiny. We were almost about to be late to the wedding, which was something I was not trying to do.

"I'm coming, baby. I'm trying to find Lil Mike's bow tie."

"I got it right here, girl, come on," I said and she ran down quickly in relief.

"Thank you, oh my God."

"Girl, you will lose your head if it was attached to your feet," I chuckled.

"Nah, that's what I got you for," she smiled and kissed me on the cheek.

I snatched Makiya up in my arms and we headed out to the limo I had rented. Once we got the kids buckled in and settled, we hopped in and made our way to the church.

"Man, drive this muthafucka!" I told the limo driver and he instantly punched the gas.

"Ring.... Ring.... Ring"

"Shit!" I cursed myself because my phone was in the pocket of my slacks and my ass was too lazy to lift up.

"Yoo!" I answered the minute I saw it was Esco.

"Blaze, have you spoke to Que?"

"Nah, not today."

"I've been calling him and his phone is just ringing."

"Man, you know Que ass he probably knee deep in some pussy," I laughed because it was the truth.

"Something is up," Esco said, sounding stressed the fuck out.

"What's wrong, Sco?" I asked and he sighed before he answered.

"That bitch he been fucking with is Mario's daughter."

259

"Wait, the bitch he brought to Nina's shower?"

"Yeah, her."

"What! You gotta be shitting me?"

"Yeah, I just did some digging and found out. Where are you?"

"I'm on my way to the wedding now."

"Ok, make sure you keep an eye out. I'm on my way there now."

"Aight, fasho."

"Blaze!" Esco called out to me.

"Yeah, I'm here."

"Don't tell Cash, please. I want her to enjoy her wedding, we will inform her and Nino after, ok?"

"Fasho," and just like that, Esco disconnected the line.

Tiny must have read my face because she was looking at me with a worried look. I was so fucked over the news that all I could do was stare at her and shake my fucking head.

After I finally got a hold of myself, I told Tiny what Esco had told me. By the time I was done, we were pulling up to the church. I quickly jumped out the limo, making sure to check my surroundings and went inside to examine the chapel.

Once I noticed everything was in tip top shape, I went back to the car to get Tiny and the kids. I walked them inside, making sure they were secure in their seats. I then pulled out my phone to dial Que and his phone only rang. I hung up and tried again but still the same results. I tried to calm my nerves and hope for the best so I went to find Nino, but making sure not to say anything because I didn't want to ruin him and Cash's moment.

Chapter 20

Cash & Nino's Wedding

Brooklyn Nino....

I sat in the room next door to Cash in the chapel where we were about to walk down the aisle. I had so much on my mind that all I could do was knock back shot after shot. Because of the marriage rule about the groom not being able to see the bride, Cash and I sat in two separate rooms, and I was glad. I was beyond stressed the fuck out. I pulled out my phone and read the text that I had got from Tiffany this morning over and over, praying to God my eyes were deceiving me.

(305) 361-6970: Nino, I'm pregnant.

Me: Man, what the fuck you mean you pregnant?

(305) 361-6970: exactly what I just said.

Me: Ok Tiff, and it ain't mine so why are you telling me?

(305) 361-6970: SMFH, you know damn well I haven't been fucking anybody but you.

Me: Man, look, you know I'm bout to get married so I'll see you in a couple days to bring you the money to handle that shit.

(305) 361-6970: Nigga, I'm not handling shit! I'm having my baby rather you like it or not! And by the way, congratulations

The more I read the text, the more I drank. This bitch knew exactly what she was doing!

She waited until the day she knew I was about to walk down the aisle to want to hit me off with the news. Deep down inside, I figured Tiffany was possibly pregnant. She had picked up some weight and all of a sudden, she had become very emotional. My heart was so hurt that I actually shed a tear. I knew this news would make Cash leave me and if that happened, I'd kill Tiffany and the baby that was growing inside of her. I knew that was some fucked up shit to say, but I couldn't lose Cash and especially to a bitch that I could never see myself with.

263

Today, I would walk down the aisle with the love of my life and drop the bombshell on her another day. I knew it was selfish of me, but I couldn't hurt Cash on the most important day of our life. Therefore, if Cash did leave me, she'd be leaving me as my wife.

I was so deep in thought that I barely heard my phone ringing. When I looked at the caller ID, I quickly answered because I saw that it was Bronx.

"Sup, bro?" I spoke, emotionally drained.

"Man, I fucked up," was all he said and I could barely understand what he was saying because it sounded like he was crying.

"Man, you crying?"

"I fucked up, Brooklyn. Man, I really fucked up," he said and indeed, he was crying.

"Where you at?"

"I'm at the Lexington Inn."

"Aight, I'll be there," I said and hung up.

I had so much shit going on that I didn't even bother to get up and go. It was one thing I needed to do and that was to walk down that aisle and make shit official with Cash. Therefore, whatever my brother was going through, it had to wait.

"It's time, Nino!" Blaze said, barging into the room.

I just looked up at him through red eyes and stood to my feet.

"Nigga, you drunk?" he asked, walking into the room and closing the door behind him.

"Hell yeah, man," I responded sluggishly, but made my way towards the door.

"Man, I don't know what's up with you but what I do know is you better sober yo ass up and meet yo bride downstairs," and with that, Blaze shut the door and left as he came.

I tried to regain my composure as I grabbed the knob. I took a deep breath and walked out the door to my wife.

Cash

"Cash, for real, do you have to take that thing?" Niya asked, looking annoyed.

"Yes, Niy, you know I don't go nowhere without Dolly, ma," I said and she just shook her head.

I looked at myself once more in the full-length mirror, I had to admit, I looked bomb as fuck. My Vera Wang dress hugged my frame, exposing my now round belly. The stomach area was full of rhinestones going up to cover my breast. The entire back was out and the bottom was sheer with an extremely long tail. My four-inch Louboutin heels matched my dress to perfection. Nikki had done my hair in an up-do with flowing curls so that my crown would fit perfectly. Brooklyn had hired the staff from Mac to slay my makeup so I was totally satisfied with my face. Before I walked out the door, I slightly bent over to make sure Dolly was secure in my rhinestone garter belt. Once I was satisfied, I walked out the door but taking a nice deep breath before. I didn't know if it was the baby or butterflies because my stomach was talking to me. I wasn't nervous about marrying Brooklyn, I was more so worried because I needed this shit to be perfect.

When I made it downstairs, I could see inside the chapel. Everyone's back was to me so they never saw me standing there. I noticed Nikki and Marvin sitting in the first few rows along with my mother. Tiny, Blaze, and Niya were sitting in the second row and across from them was Nina, Cashmere, and Carlos.

Where the fuck is Que? I thought but I quickly shook off the thought because

The moment I heard Beyonce's Dangerously in Love, I knew it was time to walk the aisle so I walked up to the door where I was now seen by the entire room. It had to be at least five hundred people in attendance and that shit really made me nervous. There were faces that I'd never seen before, but it didn't matter because I needed all the witnesses I could get.

Walking down the aisle slowly, I focused in on the decorations and they were just how I imagined. There was ice sculpture doves that had to be at least six feet. Also,

267

there were balloons that were custom made to look like glass and they read Mr. & Mrs. Carter. The ceiling changed colors, going from white to an icy blue and the lights that shimmered through it made it look like snowflakes falling down.

I looked around the room and smiled at everyone, widely. My caterers stood to the side watching me and right then, I got a leery feeling. I quickly shook it off and made my way to Brooklyn, while stood there and watched me lustfully without blinking. When I finally made it to him, he lifted the veil over my head and looked me dead in my eyes.

I know this nigga not drunk! I thought to myself but quickly let it ride because if I wasn't pregnant, I'd be drunk with his ass.

The minute the music stopped, the pastor began.

"Dearly beloved, we are gathered here today", was all I heard because I was so focused on Brooklyn who looked stressed the fuck out. Instead of smiling, he stared at me with eyes I couldn't read. They went from lust to love, and then to stress. I just prayed he wasn't regretting what he was about to do.

268

"I love you, Cash Carter," he finally spoke and made me smile. At that point, it seemed as if so much weight was lifted off my shoulders.

"I love you more, Brooklyn Nino," I said, causing him to smile.

We were so lost in each other's eyes that we almost didn't hear the chaos that was going on. Everyone was looking back and Nina was standing to her feet along with Tiny.

What the fuck going on?

I looked in the direction that everyone was looking and my eyes fell onto Tiffany. I didn't give a fuck, I was about to simply whoop her ass and then continue with my wedding. Right when I began walking towards her.

"Cash, get down!" Esco was standing in the doorway screaming with his gun drawn. When I looked in his direction, the men who were dressed as caterers had guns drawn and began to open fire.

Pow! Pow! Pow! Pow! Pow! Pow! Pow! Pow! Pow! Pow! Pow! Pow! Pow! Pow! Pow! Pow! Pow! Pow! Pow! Pow! Pow! Pow! Pow! Pow! Pow! Pow!

Pow! Pow! Pow! Pow! Pow! Pow! Pow! Pow! Pow! Pow! Pow! Pow! Pow! Pow! Pow! Pow! Pow! Pow! Pow! Pow! Pow!

Boom! Boom!

They were letting off round after round. Nino knocked me to the ground and I fell straight on my stomach. I grabbed my stomach as a reflex but I was ok, so I quickly jumped back to my feet. I then pulled Dolly out my garter belt and let off every last shot I had.

Bock! Bock! Bock! Bock! Bock! Bock! Bock! Bock! Bock! Bock! Bock! Bock! Bock! Bock! Bock! Bock! Bock! Bock! Bock! Bock! Bock! Bock! Bock! Bock! Bock! Bock! Bock! Bock! Bock! Bock! Bock! Bock! Bock! Bock! Bock! Bock! Bock! Bock! Bock! Bock! Bock! Bock! Bock! Bock! Bock! Bock! Bock! Bock!

All I could hear were the screams of the patrons and gunfire. My mother who was holding an AK 47 was bringing back the war right along with Blaze. Tiny was kneeled down shielding her kids and Nina did the same. She had the baby nestled in her arms and the car seat was laying on the side of them.

"Dad!" I yelled out when I saw Esco take a bullet and instantly hitting the ground. I started to run in his direction but when I saw him stand to his feet and run out the door, I sighed in relief. I ran out of bullets so I kneeled down for cover. From where I was I could see, Tiffany laying down the aisle and she appeared to be shot. I searched the room for Brooklyn and he was running in my direction with his gun drawn as well.

"Cash, Niya was hit!"

"What! I screamed, looking around the room in a frantic.

"Man, she dead, Cash," Brook said, shaking his head. "Come on, ma!"

"Brooklyn, I can't just leave her! Please, I have to make sure!" I shouted with tears pouring down my eyes.

"Cash, you see all these bodies. We gotta go!" again, he shouted.

He then stopped and looked down the aisle. I followed his eyes in the direction he was looking and read his lips "Tiffany."

By this time, the church was pretty much empty, except for the bodies that were sprawled all around. I grabbed Brook's guns out of his hands and tucked them under my dress because I could hear the sirens getting closer. I then tried to pull at his arm but he wouldn't budge. He looked at me and dropped his head.

"Come on, Brook!" I shouted as the paramedics were entering the chapel. He finally snapped out of it, grabbed my hand, and led me out of the church.

When I got by the door, Niya was laid out with a single shot to the head. I fell to my knees with tears pouring down my face. My friend was indeed dead and this shit killed me.

"She's pregnant!" a paramedic shouted as he rolled someone out on a stretcher.

When I looked at the body, it was Tiffany.

272

Pregnant! I looked in Brooklyn's direction when he dropped his head that was all the confirmation I needed.

"Cash, come on!" my mother yelled, knocking me out my thoughts.

I looked at Brooklyn one last time, my body said run to him but my heart wouldn't let me so I simply ran to my mother. What was supposed to be the best day of my life was the worse.

The End!

If you made it to the end of this book, I really hope I left you applaud. (smiley face) I really hope you guys enjoyed part 1 and 2. And even tho I'm gonna have to work extremely hard to please y'all with the Finale (lol) I really appreciate every single last reader and especially my Facebook readers that called me on a daily saying "are you delivering today."

Thank you to my family Bugsy, Chastity, DAnthony, Blessyn, Lil Jay, Chunks, LayLay, Miya, Cali and Dajah for allowing me the time to myself to type. Even tho yall complained about me not paying you guys any attention (lol) I love yall truly and I'm doing this for yall.

Thank you to my real friends who's still by my side since day 1 and gave me my space to type without bitching because I couldn't go out and party. #GGzzz.

Thank you to my editor Robin Chanel for the great work with editing and my dope ass covers. Sorry for making you work extra harder but you know when I'm off that henny my mind gets to going and my fingers don't stop (lol) I really appreciate you.

Thank you to everybody that pushed me further to becoming an author. Special thanks to my Mother (Girl

Toni & My Father KB). I love you Lil KB & Devonte (my big and Lil brothers) also thanks to my sponsors Kiss My Klass Clothing and Taco Gyrl Catering co.

Last but not least, I wanna thank my 30 RUz. I love every last one of my homies and homegirls to death.

Rest in Heaven My dearest Abuelita (Maria Lopez) I miss you truly my love my best friend.

Rest in Heaven (Grandma Barbara & Grandpa Curtis)

Instagram: @ AuthorBarbieScott

Facebook: Author Barbie Scott

Snap: @AutBarbieScott

Email: AuthorBarbieScott@gmail.com

The Plugs Daughter…

Be on the lookout for…

Me U & Hennessy coming Oct. 1st 2016

Trap Gyrl 3 dropping New Year's Day 2017

Barbie & Clyde dropping Feb 14th Valentine's Day 2017

Also be on the lookout for…

Nine Lives by Author Girl Toni coming soon....

Graphics by Brand Bullies Media

Facebook: Brand Bullies Media

Made in the USA
Las Vegas, NV
17 January 2021

16083279R10163